Also by Lian Tanner

A Clue for Clara
illustrated by
Cheryl Orsini

THE ROGUES
Accidental Heroes
Secret Guardians
Haunted Warriors

THE HIDDEN
Ice Breaker
Sunker's Deep
Fetcher's Song

THE KEEPERS
Museum of Thieves
City of Lies
Path of Beasts

Ella and the Ocean
illustrated by
Jonathan Bentley

RITA'S Revenge

LIAN TANNER
Illustrated by Cheryl Orsini

ALLEN&UNWIN
SYDNEY · MELBOURNE · AUCKLAND · LONDON

First published by Allen & Unwin in 2022

Copyright © Text, Lian Tanner 2022
Copyright © Illustrations, Cheryl Orsini 2022

All rights reserved. No part of this book may be reproduced or transmitted in any form or by any means, electronic or mechanical, including photocopying, recording or by any information storage and retrieval system, without prior permission in writing from the publisher. The Australian *Copyright Act 1968* (the Act) allows a maximum of one chapter or ten per cent of this book, whichever is the greater, to be photocopied by any educational institution for its educational purposes provided that the educational institution (or body that administers it) has given a remuneration notice to the Copyright Agency (Australia) under the Act.

Allen & Unwin
83 Alexander Street
Crows Nest NSW 2065
Australia
Phone: (61 2) 8425 0100
Email: info@allenandunwin.com
Web: www.allenandunwin.com

 A catalogue record for this book is available from the National Library of Australia

ISBN 978 1 76106 600 9

For teaching resources, explore
www.allenandunwin.com/resources/for-teachers

Cover and text design by Hannah Janzen
Cover illustration by Cheryl Orsini
Illustrations created in pencil and watercolour on paper
Set in 13/21 pt Archer and Gotham Narrow by Hannah Janzen

Printed in Australia in May 2022 by McPherson's Printing Group

10 9 8 7 6 5 4 3 2 1

 The paper in this book is FSC® certified. FSC® promotes environmentally responsible, socially beneficial and economically viable management of the world's forests.

www.liantanner.com.au

To Dali, Evie and Amaya,
with love

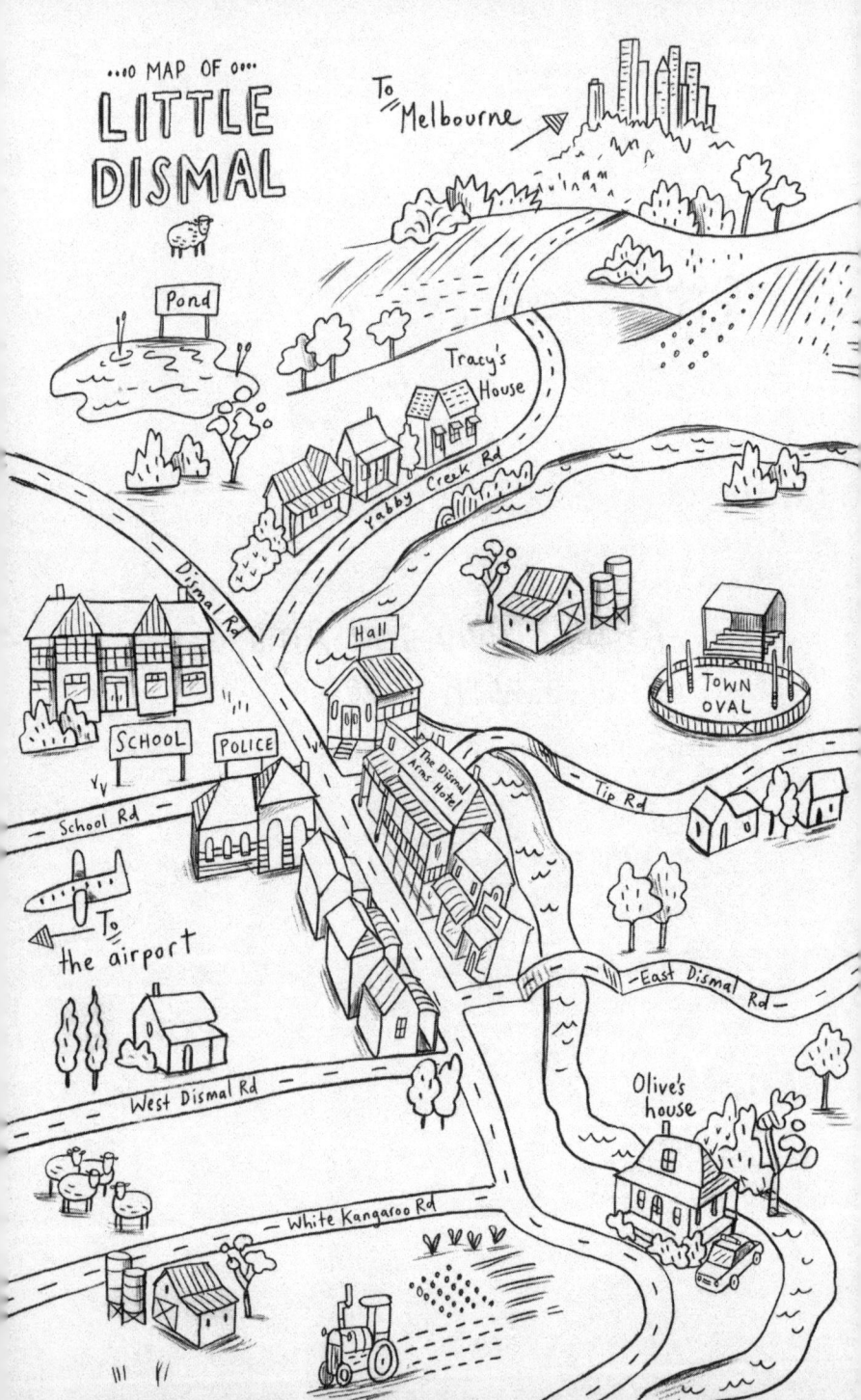

Rita's diary

Anyone can keep a diary.

Some people make an awful fuss about it, as if it makes them important and clever.

Some people.

Some *chooks*.

But keeping a diary is not hard. First you name the day.

Today

Then you name the time.

Diary o'clock

I keep my diary in my head so I don't lose it. But sometimes I like to write it on bits of paper. Here's some of my writing.

And here's some more.

They are in secret duck language, so you probably won't understand them.

I will explain.

The first one is about the courage of ducks, and how much braver and smarter we are than other birds.

Like chooks, for example.

The second one is about that last fateful Talent Night, when—

But no, I don't want to think about Talent Night.

I will go to the pond instead, and see if Great-Aunt Myrtle has forgiven me.

Pond o'clock

'So,' says Aunt Marcia. *'This chook who everyone's making such a fuss of. What's her name?'*

'Clara,' says Aunt Charlene.

'What sort of stupid name is Clara?' demands Great-Aunt Myrtle. She is so old

that all her feathers are ragged at the ends, and she can only see out of one eye. But she's still the fiercest duck in the flock. And the most important.

So I say, *'It's a chook name. A stupid chook name. Ha ha ha.'*

Great-Aunt Myrtle doesn't even glance in my direction. But the circle of empty water around me seems to grow wider. And colder.

'*People are calling her a hero,*' says Aunt Charlene, as if I haven't spoken. '*Just because she stopped the Simpson human stealing a few sheep.*'

'*Apparently she thinks she's a real detective now,*' says Aunt Deirdre.

'*I'm amazed she could even find her own feathers, much less a bunch of missing sheep,*' says Aunt Charlene. '*She's a chook, and you know what they say about chooks.*'

Everyone laughs. (I laugh loudest.)

Aunt Charlene pretends to be a chook trying to swim, and we laugh again, even though she does the exact same act at every single Talent Night—

No, I *will not* think about Talent Night.

Great-Aunt Myrtle spends a moment or two dabbling for insects, then blows a few bubbles and says, '*When I was in the lower pasture yesterday, the cows were mocking me.*'

Aunt Charlene gasps. '*What did you do?*'

'I bit their tails until they ran away.'

We all clack our beaks in approval. (I clack loudest.)

'But it's not just the cows,' Great-Aunt Myrtle continues. *'The pigs, the horses – they think we're a joke. And it's Clara's fault. She's been telling people that ducks are mad, and now every bird and beast in town is saying the same thing. And laughing. Even the humans.'*

She narrows her eyes. *'They shouldn't laugh at ducks.'*

The rest of us narrow *our* eyes, too. (My eyes are narrowest.)

My cousin Vera, over on the windmill side of the pond, cries, *'Because we know where they live!'*

At that, the aunties set up a great quack of agreement. *'Yes, we do.' 'Well said, young Vera!' 'She'll go far, that duck.'*

I wish *I* had thought of saying, *'We know where they live.'* I wish they'd quack in agreement when *I* speak. But they won't. I am in disgrace. No matter what I do, they pretend I'm not here.

Half past Vera-is-a-pain-in-the-tail-feathers

Great-Aunt Myrtle waits until the noise dies down. Then she says, *'So, it's been a while since we had a sworn enemy…'*

There are a number of words that will get a duck's immediate attention. Worms. Rain. Strawberries.

Sworn enemy.

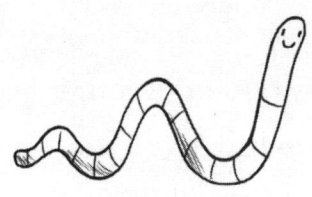

Every duck on the pond (including me) stiffens.

'You mean—' says Aunt Marcia.

'Revenge,' says Great-Aunt Myrtle. *'On Clara.*

For telling lies about us. For saying we are mad, when we are not.'

Aunt Deirdre flaps her wings. *'Excellent idea. We'll make that chook's life a misery.'*

'When do we start?' asks Aunt Charlene.

Aunt Marcia clears her throat. *'I'm all for revenge, Myrtle. And of course it's your decision. But Clara has friends in very high places these days.'*

There's a moment of silence. Then Aunt Charlene says, *'We can't let that stop us. I'd go after her, but I did the last one, and it seems dreadfully unfair that I should have all the fun.'*

'I wish I could do it,' says Aunt Deirdre, *'but my ducklings are about to hatch.'*

'I would lead the way myself,' says Great-Aunt Myrtle. *'But I have to pay back an insult from the pigs on the Waddle farm. I've left it far too long already.'*

They look at each other. They look at my

cousins. Everyone suddenly develops an interest in the algae that floats under the surface of the water.

Everyone except me.

This-is-my-chance o'clock

I might have disgraced myself beyond bearing. I might have done something so un-duck-ish that no one will even look at me.

But there's a way back, and I have just seen it.

I take my fate in my beak and say loudly, *'I'll do it.'*

'Who was that?' demands Great-Aunt Myrtle, dropping a clump of algae.

'It's Rita,' says Aunt Charlene. *'The one who thinks she's a poet.'*

'Not anymore,' I say quickly. *'That thing at Talent Night was just an accident…'*

They're not listening. Great-Aunt Myrtle says, without looking at me, *'Ducks cannot be poets.*

*It's not on the list of approved activities.'

'Why on earth,'* demands Aunt Marcia, *'would anyone want to do something that's not on the list? Tell them, Myrtle.'*

List o'clock

Great-Aunt Myrtle waddles up onto the bank and strikes the Pose of Wisdom.

I have tried to do the Pose of Wisdom, but it's harder than it looks. You have to stand on one leg, and stretch out the other leg and your wing at exactly the right angle without falling over.

I fell over.

Perhaps I should have taken it as a sign.

'Pay attention, all of you.' Despite her age, Great-Aunt Myrtle is

so well balanced that she doesn't even wobble. *'Here is the list of approved activities, handed down from the beginning of time.'*

Even the smallest ducklings paddling in the shallows lift their heads and listen.

'Dabbling, diving and preening,' recites Great-Aunt Myrtle. *'Flapping and foraging. Flying, hissing and biting.'*

By now, we're all reciting with her. My voice is the loudest, but still they take no notice of me. *'Chasing cows and pigs. Mockery. Rude songs. Piracy, bullying, revenge, warfare and general thuggery.'*

'What about murder?' asks one of the ducklings. *'Are we allowed to do murder?'*

'Only if the other person deserves it,' says Great-Aunt Myrtle.

'Which they usually do,' adds Aunt Marcia.

Great-Aunt Myrtle folds her tattered wing, then stretches it out again to emphasise her point. *'Please note that poetry is nowhere on the list. It's not at the beginning, it's not in the middle, and it's not at the end. There is not even the slightest hint of poetry. Which means—'*

Now at last she turns to glare at me. *'Which means that we do not do it.'*

I blush under my feathers. But at least she's taking notice of me.

'Let me be the one,' I beg. *'Let me take revenge on our sworn enemy.'*

Aunt Marcia and Aunt Deirdre go into a huddle, whispering to each other. Aunt Charlene paddles around me in circles, muttering under her breath.

Great-Aunt Myrtle doesn't move.

'I'll wreak a really good revenge,' I tell her. *'Something that will make everyone sit up and take notice. Something that will teach them not to laugh at ducks.'*

Aunt Charlene looks thoughtful. *'Maybe we should give her a chance.'*

'No,' snaps Great-Aunt Myrtle. *'I'll send someone reliable. Like Vera.'*

On the other side of the pond, Vera flaps her wings enthusiastically and begins to paddle towards the aunties.

I block her way. *'I'll be* so *reliable,'* I say.

But Great-Aunt Myrtle just dips her beak in the water, tilts her head back and takes a drink, as if the matter is settled.

Desperation o'clock

If I miss this chance, my life is as good as over. No one will ever swim beside me again. No one will look at me. No one will talk to me. I will be the loneliest duck in the world.

So I tuck my wings tightly against my body and cry, *'I don't want to be a poet. I hate poetry! It's not on the list. Ducks can't be poets.'*

Something inside my chest hurts when I say those words, but I ignore it. Because Great-

Aunt Myrtle's head whips back around and she stares at me. *'Do you mean it?'*

'Yes!'

'We could let her try.' Aunt Charlene waggles her tail feathers. *'It can be a test.'*

'Yes, a test,' says Aunt Marcia. *'And if she fails…'*

'Or if she commits poetry…' mutters Great-Aunt Myrtle.

'… Then we know where she lives,' cries Vera.

'Yes, we do.' 'Well said, youngster,' quack the aunties. *'She'll go far, that Vera.'*

I hardly hear them. I'm already thinking ahead, trying to work out what I can do to Clara.

It'll take me a while to sort out the details. But whatever it is, it's going to be spectacular.

It's going to be amazing.

And it's going to make every duck in the town of Little Dismal forget that I once wanted to be a poet.

Still today

Happiness o'clock

As I fly away from the pond, the wind catches my wings and ruffles my feathers. I am on a mission for Great-Aunt Myrtle! Soon I will be part of the flock again!

Happiness wells up inside me
as warm and beautiful
as a new-laid egg—

STOP! I almost fall out of the sky in horror. That was the beginnings of a poem!
What's wrong with me?

Quickly, I glance down at my shadow on the ground below. Does it look like an arrow of vengeance, swooping across the landscape? Does it look fierce? Does it look relentless?

No.

I stiffen my neck. I narrow my eyes (but then I have to widen them again, because I can't see where I'm going). I adjust my flight pattern so that my shadow spells out a warning to anyone who crosses me.

I am a duck, and ducks don't write poetry.

Not ever.

So … maybe it wasn't really a poem. Maybe it was just indigestion from eating breakfast too quickly.

Even Great-Aunt Myrtle couldn't object to a bit of indigestion.

Half past definitely-no-poetry

My mission of revenge leads me to the building that humans call 'school'.

It is still early, and Clara is not here yet.

But she should be arriving soon.

I crouch behind a rock, where she will not see me, and wait.

Ducks are very patient.

...

Ducks are *fairly* patient.

...

This is ridiculous. Where is she?

Someone-is-coming o'clock

I hear someone approaching, and I crouch lower. Is it my target? Is it Clara?

No. It is a small flock of human children carrying bags. I watch from behind the rock as they put their bags on the ground and begin to chase each other.

More children arrive.

And more.

And now at last I hear a squawk! Clara is coming!

Don't-get-too-excited o'clock

As a duckling, I studied the teachings of the famous general Ya Wu, who once led her small squad of ducks to victory against an entire battalion of feral pigs.

The teachings of General Ya

1. Let your plans be as dark and mysterious as the inside of a cow.
2. Before you move, get to know your enemy as well as you know your own egg.
3. Then fall upon them like an enraged auntie, and victory is assured.

Right now, my plans *are* as dark and mysterious as the inside of a cow. The trouble is, they are dark and mysterious to *me*. I don't think that's what General Ya meant.

And it's not yet time to fall upon Clara like an enraged auntie.

So today I am getting to know her.

The first thing I notice is that she is not alone. She rides into the schoolyard on the front of a two-wheel, with a human girl pedalling. When the two-wheel stops, Clara flutters to the ground, and the other children gather around her.

Their eagerness reminds me of something.

What is it?

It reminds me—

It reminds me of General Ya and her faithful troops!

Clara has *her own human army!*

(This is not usual for a chook.)

'Hey, Clara,' says one of the children, 'tell us how you stole Jubilee Simpson's phone.'

Clara bends over a small blue object on the ground, and starts pecking at it. What is she doing? The blue object does not look edible. Why would you peck something that's not edible?

Unless she's trying to kill it. In which case,

she's taking an awfully long time.

Another of the children bends over the blue object and says, '"When ... Jubilee Crystal Simpson ... put her phone ... on the car seat ... I snatched it up ... and ran for my life."'

'What about the truck?' says the first child. 'Tell us about the truck.'

'"Mr Simpson ... was trying to escape ... with the stolen sheep ... so I hid ... in the back ... of the truck."'

The rest of the children make admiring noises. One of them says, 'That's so cool that Clara's got her own phone, Olive. And that she can use it to talk to us.'

Wait, Clara is *talking* to the humans?

I didn't know that was possible.

I mean, we all understand the language; we learn it as ducklings, along with unarmed combat and the art of warfare.

And humans can be a lot of fun. You can chase them, attack them, give them the death stare. You can bite their children, their ankles and their dogs.

But I've never heard of anyone actually *talking* to them.

'She's really clever,' says the girl called Olive. 'She knows semaphore and Morse code, don't you, Clara?'

What are these strange words? What is semaphore? What is Morse code?

And why would anyone say, 'She's really clever' without adding 'for a chook'?

I crouch behind my rock, thinking hard.

Clara's troops seem very loyal. So when the time comes for me to fall upon her like an enraged auntie, they will probably defend her.

I do not think I can fight them all.

Hmmm, perhaps I need my own human army…

Half past where-is-my-army?
On the other side of the playground, a girl

is sitting alone, with her back turned to her fellow humans.

She does not seem to be part of Clara's army.

Which means she can be mine.

It's time to try this talking-to-humans thing.

I creep around the edge of the playground until I'm standing in front of her. She's small for a human, with dark hair and an unhappy face. (That will change when she hears the good news.)

'*Congratulations, human,*' I say.

She jumps, as if she wasn't expecting the great honour of being spoken to by a duck.

'*I have chosen you to take part in my grand plan of revenge,*' I tell her. '*You will not be making any important decisions, but I will train you in unarmed combat, and at my command you will fight your fellow humans. You will also:*

1. *Answer my questions.*
2. *Watch my revenge.*
3. *Admire my revenge.*

4. *Spread the word about my revenge to other humans so they know not to laugh at ducks.*

So, have you got all that?'

She glares at me, and mutters, 'Quack quack quack to you too, duck.'

'My name is Rita. But you can call me Captain Rita.'

'Quack quack,' says my new army. 'I heard you the first time.'

She still looks unhappy. Perhaps she did not understand me properly.

'Listen carefully,' I say. *'I am here for revenge.'*

'Quack quack.'

'Revenge. Say it after me.'

'Quack. This is getting boring.'

'Re-venge.'

My army sighs. 'How stupid is this? I'm talking to a duck.'

'No you're not. You're not even trying. Let's start again—'

I am interrupted by a dreadful noise. It sounds as if the school has come under attack by goats.

My army stands up.

'Where are you going?' I ask her.

She doesn't answer. Instead, she walks towards the school building, behind Clara and her army.

'Listen,' I say, running alongside her. *'We need to get started with your training. I suggest we go down to the river and practise some kicks … No? All right then, I'll come with you into "school", and we can—'*

She opens the door.

'You don't want to start the kicks today? Not a problem. But you are my army, right?'

'Yeah yeah, duck,' she says.

'Excellent! In that case, I'll come with you and—'

The door shuts in my face.

Still today
(the same one)

What-do-I-do-now o'clock

How can I get to know my sworn enemy if I can't see her?

How can I train my army if I can't bite her?

I decide to follow them.

The door refuses to open, even when I give it the death stare. So I scout around the back of the school, tossing a few insults at the school chooks as I pass their pen.

And there it is! A hole in the wall, just big enough for a duck.

I launch myself into the air, quick and stealthy. I fly straight through the hole and into the—

OW!!!!!!!

The hole is not a hole.

As I lie on the ground beneath it, I remember Aunt Charlene telling us about something called 'glass'.

I think I have just met it.

Half past glass

I lie there until my beak stops hurting. A couple of magpies fly overhead, and I pretend I'm hunting for worms.

When they are out of sight, I peer up at the glass. If I flew at it with twice the speed, could I force it open?

No. One of General Ya's most famous sayings is, 'Avoid what is strong and strike at what is weak.'

The glass is strong.

What is weak?

The school chooks? Perhaps I could throw one of *them* at the glass…

No, I don't think that would work.

Hmm.

General Ya also said, 'If you wish to invade the pigsty, you must fool the pigs into thinking you are going to attack the cowshed...'

Sneaky o'clock

The school chookpen has trees on one side and a wire fence all around it. I fly some distance away, catch an air current and glide back to the trees, as silent as a dead frog.

Below me, the chooks are going about their morning business. Most of them are taking dust baths, but a few have moved on to hunting for earwigs.

I wait until two of them are almost directly under the tree.

Then I say, in a low voice, *'So what's the plan?'*

In a *different* voice (based on Aunt Marcia) I answer myself. *'Wait until they are all in a bunch. Then we attack from above.'*

The chooks' heads jerk up. They stare around. I rustle the leaves, then hop over to another branch and rustle some more.

One of the chooks stares up at the trees and nudges the other with her wing. *'Ducks,'* she whispers. *'Listen.'*

'What about the wire over the top of the pen?' I say.

'There's a hole in the corner,' I reply in my Aunt Marcia voice. *'We'll dive through it and attack before they know what's hit them.'*

There's no hole in the corner of the wire, but the chooks don't even check. Instead, they squawk at the tops of their voices, *'Spike! Spike! The ducks are coming to attack us!'*

Their rooster, who was stretched out in a dust bath, leaps to his feet and comes tearing over. *'What? Where are they?'*

'Up in the tree! Up in the tree!' cry the chooks.

It's hard to make myself heard over the noise they are making, but I shout, *'AND*

ONCE WE'RE IN THE PEN, WE'LL CALL IN THE FOXES.'

'*Foxes?*' Spike's shriek of alarm is so loud it nearly deafens me. '*Ladies!*' he cries. '*Back to the coop! Bar the door! Top perch only! No dawdlers! Tuck your legs up! Hurry! Hurry! Hurry!*'

The chooks run for their lives, still squawking. Spike prowls the edges of the pen, his feathers puffed up to twice his usual size. His neck is curved in fury. His spurs gleam.

'*Where are you, foxes?*' he shrieks. '*Show yourselves, you stinking red dogs. I'll tear you apart!*'

I take one last look at the chaos before I glide out of the tree, making sure Spike doesn't see me.

As soon as I'm out of sight of the chookpen, I race around to the front of the school, and get there just as an adult human sticks her head out the door.

I dive behind another rock.

A voice from inside the school calls out, 'Hey Daphne, why are the chooks making that awful racket?'

'Might be a snake,' says Daphne. 'I'd better go and check.'

She hurries out the door, which begins to swing closed behind her. I make a dash for it, and get through the gap just in time.

Half past more-sneaking

I have never been inside a human building before. But I have heard about them from Aunt Charlene's stories. So I was expecting the strangeness.

But still I feel as if the sky has dropped down far too close, and someone has stolen all the earth and grass and left nothing behind but nasty flat rock, which I believe is called a floor.

Hard sky above me
hard floor below me

already I am missing
the squish of worms
and the soft
friendly puddle
of—

STOP!
NO!
NO NO NO!
I march across the floor, muttering, *'Ducks do not write poetry. Which means I do not write poetry! So that wasn't a poem, it was a description—'*

That's when I notice a room with glass across the front of it. Standing in front of the glass are two humans – one big and one small.

The small human is looking at me.

'Duck,' it says.

I dive under a four-legged thing.

The big human turns around. 'What was that, Chloe?'

'Duck,' says the small human, pointing at me.

'No, darling, that's a chair. Can you say *chair?*'

Behind me, the front door opens again and Daphne comes in. 'No sign of anything,' she says. 'Maybe a hawk flew overhead. Anyway, they're calming down now. I'll let them out for their morning scratch soon.'

While she's talking, I slip out from under the chair and race down the corridor.

'Duck!' screams the small human.

No one takes any notice. I have infiltrated the enemy's headquarters undetected.

Where-is-my-sworn-enemy o'clock

I creep through the school, diving for cover whenever I hear humans. Legs hurry past me as I crouch behind a door. Feet almost trample me when I hide under a rug.

To my surprise, there are several armies

gathered here. In one room they appear to be drawing up battle plans on large sheets of paper. In another, they are experimenting with strange weapons.

I sneak past them, searching for Clara – and find her in a room at the far end of the building, with her army seated all around her.

If I stay in the doorway for long, I will be spotted. But there is a box next to it, with a flap on top. I nudge the flap a little wider and dive inside.

The flap closes, leaving just enough room for me to see out.

Hehehehehehehehe.

I spy on Clara.
I spy on her army.
I spy on *my* army, who is sitting by herself at the back of the room, writing on a piece of paper.

I expect she is describing our first meeting, and the thrill of being chosen by a duck.

Thursday
Little Dismal

To Jubilee Crystal Simpson
Somewhere on earth

Hi Jubilee! I was going to text you, but Mum took my phone away. She says you're a bad influence and I'm not allowed to talk to you. She says you must have known all along that your dad was stealing sheep.

So I told her you didn't know anything about it. Because you didn't. Did you?

Anyway, that's why I'm writing a letter instead of texting.

School's horrible without you here. Everyone

hates me except Mrs Savage, who has to like me because she's our teacher. But I bet she secretly hates me too.

And everyone's sucking up to Olive Hennessey, because her pet chook Clara was the one who got your dad arrested.

I hate Olive Hennessey. I hate her pet chook and her cousin Digby. I hate everyone except you.

Mum says you were never really my friend, and that you just used me. But I know that's not true.

I hate Mum, too. And my stepdad Laurie. And I'm pretty sure they hate me and wish they only had the ~~twins~~ brats.

Anyway, Laurie's got this new job, fly-in fly-out, so he's away for a couple of weeks at a time. Which is good, because he's horrible, just like you said.

I wish my real dad was here, instead of in Queensland. I wish I knew your address, so I could post this. Then you could write back. You would write back, wouldn't you?

Love from your best friend Tracy

PS. We've got this really stupid homework. We have to write an acrostic poem about friendship, using the word FRIEND. Like this.

Friendship is stupid
Really stupid
I haven't got any friends except you
Everyone else hates me
No one likes me
Do I care? No.

Except I can't hand that in, because Mrs Savage would have a talk with me. Remember her talks?

Yeah, me too.

We've got a couple of weeks before it's due. Maybe I'll say I did the homework, but the brats ate it. Ha ha.

Still today
still the same one

Spying-on-my-sworn-enemy o'clock

There is an adult female standing at the front of the room. One of Clara's troops calls her Mrs Savage.

'This afternoon,' says Mrs Savage, 'we are having a visitor. Ms Delphine Murray is a journalist writing an article about growing up in a small country town. Olive, I think you have something to say?'

Olive stands up. 'Please don't tell the journalist about Clara. If news gets out about how clever she is, she won't be able to go undercover anymore.'

There they go again, saying Clara is clever. And they're all nodding – except for my army, who is scowling and saying nothing.

I'm glad I chose her.

'I kind of wish we *could* tell everyone about her,' says the boy sitting next to Olive. 'I mean, it's an amazing story.'

'It is, Digby,' says Mrs Savage.

'Imagine people's faces,' says Digby, 'if they knew that Clara helped Constable Hennessey catch Mr Simpson. And that she keeps a diary.'

'Oh my word, I didn't know about the diary.' Mrs Savage sits down with a thump.

'She's really good at writing,' says Olive.

Digby laughs. 'Imagine if I told the journalist that you've got a chook who keeps a diary. She'd think I was mad.'

And suddenly, the entire room (except for my army) says in chorus, 'You're not a duck, Digby.'

They seem to think this is funny.

It is not funny.

Half past hiding-in-the-box

I wait until everyone has gone outside for something called 'last football practice before the big match'.

(I was hoping that my army would stay behind so we could get started on unarmed combat. But she goes with them.)

Then I sneak out of my box and find a piece of paper. And a pen.

That one broke.

I find another pen.

That one broke too.

I find another pen.

These pens were obviously made by chooks. A pen that was made by ducks would not break so easily.

I find one that lasts a little longer.

Clara is not the only one who is good at writing.

HOMEWORK SHEET – MATHS

Digby Carella

1. Work out 0.7 + 0.9
2. Write the Roman numeral XXXVIII in figures
3. I have $15. I spend $2.50. How much have I got left?
4. A piece of wood measuring 4 m is cut into eight equal lengths. How long will each bit be?
5. What is 28 multiplied by 103?
6. Write down a multiple of 7 between 40 and 50.
7. Evie's and Dylan's ages add up to 19. Evie is 3 years older than Dylan. How old are they?
8. $\frac{2}{3} + \frac{1}{6} =$
9. There is a 50% discount on an item that costs $200. What is the new cost of the item?
10. Add 15 minutes to 1:05 PM.

Quarter past writing

I leave my writing at the front of the room, to impress Clara's army. Then I search their bags for something to eat.

What I eat

*A squishy sandwich
an apple
little white seeds
that crunch in my beak
a very small pen
something shiny
that might have tasted nice
but didn't
and another sandwich.*

This is not a poem. This is a list.

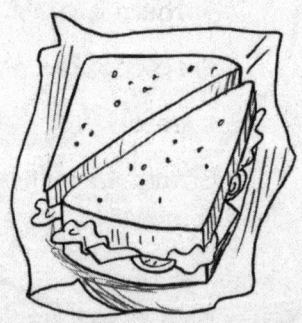

Half past eating

I'm heading towards the front door of the school to do some more spying, when I see something that stops me in my tracks.

My sworn enemy stands alone in the middle of an empty room.

Alone and undefended!

General Ya was wrong. I don't need to get to know Clara. I don't need dark and mysterious plans.

I don't even need my human army.

I will fall upon this pesky chook like an enraged auntie. And I will do it now.

Revenge o'clock!

The bite of a duck is a magnificent thing.

If you're a duck.

If you're not a duck, it is terrifying. When Clara sees me racing at her with my neck outstretched, she will leap in the air with fright, and run away as fast as she can.

But she will not escape my glorious revenge.

(My only regret is that Great-Aunt Myrtle is not here to witness my triumph.)

I settle my feathers. I take aim. I race towards my sworn enemy.

I am almost upon her when she looks up from her phone and says, *'Two PM tomorrow.'*

This is so unexpected that I skid to a halt. *'What?'*

'Whatever it is, I can't do it before then,' says Clara. *'I'm still investigating the Case of the Missing Vegemite Sandwich. I expect to have it solved by this afternoon, but then I'm going undercover at the Co-op. Two PM tomorrow is the earliest I can get to you.'*

She thinks I have come to her for help!

'I am not one of your clients,' I snap. *'My name is Rita, and I'm here for revenge.'*

'I don't take revenge cases,' says Clara. *'Too messy. But if you've got a missing duckling…'*

Her phone buzzes like a mosquito. She taps

it with her beak and says, '*A lead. Sorry, I have to go.*'

She picks up her phone with her beak and tucks it in the small bag that hangs around her neck.

Then she bustles away, leaving me standing alone in the middle of the room.

I am glad Great-Aunt Myrtle isn't here.

Why are chooks wrong?
They are the wrong shape.
Their beaks are wrong.
Their feet are wrong.
They can't swim.
They can't fly very far.
They are not ducks.

This is also a list.

Thursday afternoon
Little Dismal

To Jubilee Crystal Simpson
Somewhere on earth

Hey Jubilee, you would've liked the class visitor we had this afternoon. She was really pretty, and she dresses like a model or something.

She said she wants to get to know Little Dismal, so she's going to be here for a couple of weeks. She wants to get to know us, too, so she can write an article about us.

Mrs Savage told us that we had to get permission from our parents to talk to her. So I will. But I'll wait until the brats' bedtime, when Mum's not listening properly. She'll agree to anything then.

Isn't Delphine a cool name? It's almost as nice as Jubilee.

My name's boring. I think I'm going to change it.

Love from your best friend ~~Tracy~~ Celeste

PS. Want to hear something stupid? I've got a pet duck. It followed me home from school today.

Don't tell Mum, but I'm going to keep it.

Maybe it's a detective, like Clara.

Ha ha, not really.

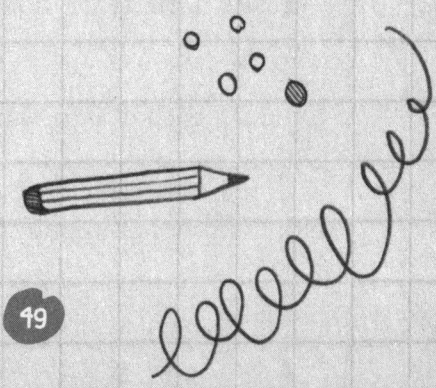

Today
(the same one)

Half past arrival

General Ya was right. I need dark and mysterious plans. I need to get to know my enemy before I fall upon her.

I also need a well-trained human army.

Unarmed combat was one of my favourite lessons when I was a duckling. In fact, Aunt Deirdre once told me that I was the best pupil she'd had for ages, even better than cousin Vera.

Of course, that was before the Talent Night incident—

No, I will *not* think about Talent Night.

'We're going to start with the basics,' I say to my army.

She is lying on her nest (which she calls a 'bed'). It is not nearly as nice as the nests at home, but it will do for now. Later, I will teach her to gather twigs and grass and build something better. Perhaps we can even make a small pond.

But first, a lesson in unarmed combat—

Wait. Her eyes are closed. How can she learn anything if she doesn't watch me?

I explain that she must watch.

'Ow!' she cries. 'You bit me!'

She is now watching carefully.

'The first thing you must learn is distance,' I tell her. *'If you're too close to the enemy, they can peck you or strike you with their wings.'*

I advance up the nest to show her what I mean by 'too close'.

She backs away from me.

Excellent, she has already learnt the first lesson.

'*Next,*' I say, '*we think about positioning. You must be confident and alert. Don't slump. Don't look weak. Carry your head high and your wings tucked neatly against your body. Like this.*'

I demonstrate what I mean, hoping she will copy me.

She doesn't. She is still watching, but she remains slumped.

I advance on her again, and she squeaks and scrambles upright.

Now she looks alert.

'*Very good,*' I say. (According to General Ya, it is important to praise your troops when they get something right.)

She is doing so well that I move straight on to kicks, blocks and biting.

'*Imagine your enemy is coming at you,*' I say. '*You block their attack like this.*'

I raise my wing to ward off an imaginary blow.

'Then, while they are still surprised, you pivot on one foot—' I demonstrate *'—kick their legs out from under them, and bite them as hard as you can.'*

I finish with the Victorious Warrior pose. It is a lot easier than the Pose of Wisdom, which is just as well, because it is not a good idea to fall over in front of your army.

She stares at me with wide eyes. 'Wow!'

I dip my head modestly. *'Would you like to see it again in slow motion? Yes? So, your enemy is coming at you with evil intentions—'*

I run through the whole thing again, and my army watches closely. By the time I finish, her eyes are even wider.

'That is amazing,' she whispers. Then she grabs a paper and pen from her nest-side table and begins to write.

I expect she is recording my instructions so she doesn't forget them. Or perhaps she is writing her memoir, like General Ya. This moment will clearly be the highlight.

Thursday afternoon
Little Dismal

To Jubilee Crystal Simpson

Somewhere on earth

Hey Jubilee! Guess what? Go on, try and guess. Except you won't be able to. You'll never ever get it.

My pet duck *dances!*

No, really. You should have seen her just now. It was the funniest thing, she was waving her wings and kicking out her legs, and I almost burst out laughing.

But then it didn't seem funny at all.

I mean, it was.

But it wasn't.

Cos you know how Mum said she was going to arrange for me to have dancing lessons? With that teacher in Yabby Creek?

Well, she forgot.

I bet she wouldn't forget if the brats wanted dancing lessons. I bet she'd sign them up as soon as they asked.

Except they wouldn't ask for dancing lessons. They'd ask for how-can-we-make-more-noise lessons. Or how-can-we-break-more-of-our-sister's-stuff lessons.

Ha ha.

Not that I care about the dancing or anything. It'd probably be really boring. If you were still here we could go along together and laugh at them.

Love from your best friend Celeste

P.S. I wish you'd said goodbye before you left.

~~P.P.S. I wish Dad would phone. Or write. Or something.~~

~~P.P.P.S. I wish everyone didn't hate me.~~

Today
The same one

Quarter past unarmed-combat

My army is trying to build me a pond. I appreciate the thought, but she's doing it all wrong.

For a start, she's trying to build it right in the middle of her nest. And she's getting the water *from her eyes*.

I wouldn't believe it if I hadn't seen it for myself. But there it is, water running down her face and dripping onto the nest.

Aunt Charlene has told us about taps. My army must have a tap in her head.

But it is not a very good one. And the

water isn't even staying on the surface. It's soaking in.

How long does she think this is going to take?

'Maybe we should get some clay,' I suggest. *'Spread it over the nest. A nice thick layer. That'll hold the water better.'*

She doesn't answer. She just keeps dripping.

How would General Ya handle this situation? I don't think it ever came up in our lessons, so I decide to use my initiative. The pond is obviously not going to happen, but it's a pity to waste the water.

I move in closer to catch the drips as they roll down my army's face. She drops her memoir and throws her arms around me.

I freeze in shock. Is this an attack? Should I slide out of her grip, then pivot and kick?

I'm just about to make my move when she wails in my ear, 'You're the only one who likes me, duck.'

Right. I don't think she's attacking me.

The water is still running down her face, so I keep drinking. This might come in handy if there's another drought.

But then I hear footsteps.

My army rubs the water from her eyes and hisses, 'Shhhhh!' And she shoves me under the nest, along with her memoir.

What just happened? Why did she hiss at me? Has she been associating with geese?

Or was *this* an attack, and she is really a spy sent by Clara?

Cautiously, I stick my head out. She hisses again, puts her finger to her lips, and says, 'I know you don't understand me, but shhh! It's Mum. Stay under the bed.'

Ah, but I *do* understand. *Mum* is the spy.

I stay under the bed.

Mum o'clock

Someone knocks on the door, and an adult

female enters, closely followed by two small males.

One of these three is Mum-the-spy, but I don't know which one.

The small ones throw themselves onto the nest, screaming, 'Tacy! Tacy!' The nest bounces alarmingly above my head.

'Hi Trace,' says the adult female.

'Don't call me that,' mumbles my army. 'My name's Celeste.'

'Yeah? Uh – oka-ay.'

'Lest!' shrieks one of the small humans.

'Lest lest!' screams the other.

'I ran into Mrs Savage this afternoon,' says the adult female, 'and she told me you're not playing in the match against Yabby Creek tomorrow.'

The nest squeaks, and a small face peers over the side. 'Duck,' it whispers.

'I mean, it's up to you, of course. But you used to love football—'

'No, I didn't,' says my army. 'It's a stupid game.'

Another face appears beside the first. 'Duck!'

I raise my wings and prepare for battle. But before I can deliver my first kick, my army leaps off the nest and says, 'I've got to do homework. Go away, boys.'

And she pushes them out the door.

The adult female lingers. I think this must be Mum-the-spy. 'Listen, Trace – I mean Celeste. About your dad—'

'La la la homework la la la,' sings my army.

Mum-the-spy sighs and leaves. I sit under the nest and go over what I have learnt about humans so far.

1. They are simple creatures who cannot understand duck language.
2. But they can be trained.
3. They have taps in their eyes (handy for drought).
4. The small ones are very loud.

I'm not sure how this will help me with Clara. But at least we have made a start on the unarmed combat.

Today
(But a different today from the last one)

Half past egg

I'm trying to get my army into a strict early-morning training regime. But she refuses to understand me.

'Fly seven laps of the backyard,' I say.

Then I remember that she can't fly.

'Run seven laps of the backyard,' I tell her. *'Seven laps. SEVEN LAPS.'*

Then I remember that she can't speak Duck.

I look around for some way of explaining it to her.

I find it.

I race for the door.

Training o'clock

My army runs seven laps of the backyard, hissing, 'Bring back my hairbrush, you stupid duck!' all the way.

Half past training

Mum-the-spy is bustling around the house.

Who is she spying for? Clara? The magpies? *Vera?*

I keep out of sight, just in case.

School o'clock

My army goes to school on her two-wheel, and I fly high above her.

Today is another get-to-know-your-enemy day. I will follow Clara and her army into the school, and—

But this morning, they do not go into the school. Instead, they wait outside until a large motor thing arrives, and another human army spills out of it.

Clara's army faces the new arrivals and shouts, 'Little Dismal for the win! Hooray!'

The new arrivals stamp their feet. 'Yabby Creek, Yabby Creek, hoo hoo hoo!'

In the middle of her army, Clara squawks and flaps her wings.

The children march out of the schoolyard,

across the road and down another road. I skulk after them, keeping out of sight.

(Ducks are excellent at skulking.)

A little way down this road they turn onto something called an oval. Some of the children stand around the edges, while others gather in the middle.

I hide behind a fence. My heart is beating fast. This reminds me of the time Great-Aunt Myrtle declared war against the ducks of Greater Dismal Swamp.

Except there is no swamp.

And I am the only duck.

War o'clock

This is a very strange war. Mrs Savage puts a silver thing in her mouth and makes a whistling sound. But instead of attacking each other, both armies *attack a ball*.

What's more, the watching children are screaming with excitement. Even though there is no bloodshed.

What *is* going on?

I decide to watch for a little longer before I make my move...

Half past watching

That's long enough. These people can't even kill a ball without help. And Clara, who is squawking on the sidelines, makes no effort to teach them.

Pathetic.

I will show them how to do it. When they see how superior I am, they will beg to join my army instead of Clara's.

And she will be left defenceless.

Friday night
Little Dismal

To Jubilee Crystal Simpson
Somewhere on earth

Hi Jubilee! Guess what? Delphine Murray asked me to show her around Little Dismal!!!!!!!!!!

I ran into her on my way home from school today, and she said she hoped I wasn't too busy, because she'd noticed me in class and thought I might be just the right person to help her.

She asked about my family, so I told her about Dad being stuck in Queensland, and how he can't get back to visit me even though he'd really like to. Then she asked if I had any uncles or aunts, so I told her how Constable Hennessey arrested Dad's brother Dylan and sent him to jail for no reason at all.

Delphine thought that was awful, and she knows this organisation called the Innocence Project that gets people out of jail when they've been wrongly convicted. She promised to write to them about Uncle Dylan!

So then we walked up one side of the main street and down the other (it took 5 minutes ha ha) and she was really interested in the police station and the Co-op and the shops, even though they're all boring and old-fashioned like you said. And she called me Celeste *every time.*

Mum keeps calling me Trace, though I told her not to. I think maybe she tried a couple of times, but then she forgot again. If she cared about me, she'd call me the name I want to be called by.

I was going to tell Mum about the Innocence Project, but Delphine said I should keep it to myself for now, because that'll make it a really cool surprise when the truth comes out.

Except Mum won't think it's cool. She doesn't like Uncle Dylan because he's my real dad's brother. But I didn't tell Delphine that.

I bet her family is really happy. I bet they all love each other and are nice to each other. And none of them ever got divorced, or ~~went away to Queensland and forgot about their daughter~~ had to put up with a horrible stepdad.

Love from your best friend Celeste.

PS. My duck followed me to school today. We were watching the footy match against Yabby Creek – and no, I wasn't playing. It's a stupid game, like you said. I know people reckon you weren't really American, but you were. I mean, you are. And American football is really cool the way you described it, and I wish we could play that instead.

Anyway, Jessica Abood was just about to

take a mark, when my duck flew right in front of her and attacked the ball like some sort of miniature gladiator.

Everyone froze on the spot. Who was going to win, the duck or the ball?

Well, I'll tell you. My duck won. The ball went flat and bits of leather flew everywhere, and the duck attacked them, too.

It was so cool!

PPS. I probably wouldn't tell you this if you were really going to read it. But sometimes I feel like that duck. I just want to attack something and tear it to pieces.

Yeah, stupid, I know.

A different today
Again!

Half past egg

Keeping a diary is not as easy as I thought. How do I tell the days apart, if it's always today?

I expect Clara also has this trouble.

I will have to find a solution.

Meanwhile, I'm basking in my victory against the ball. It was a tricky enemy, but I beat it, and Clara's army was awed by my strength and intelligence. I expect they are beginning to understand just how superior ducks are.

Unfortunately, they did not desert Clara, as I had hoped. Perhaps she has some sort of hold over them. I'll have to find out what it is.

Disappointment o'clock

My army is refusing to learn unarmed combat. I show her the moves again, but she just makes a sad face. How can she fight Clara's army if she does not have the skills?

I get her to run around the backyard twelve times, to make up for it.

Half past training

Still hiding from Mum-the-spy. She hasn't seen me yet.

The two small humans are a different matter. They turn up in unexpected places, and have already spotted me once this morning.

'Duck!' they scream.

My army puts something called 'mandarin' into their mouths to keep them quiet.

Mandarin is a breed of duck. But the small ones are not eating a duck. (I checked.)

Humans are confusing.

School o'clock

I'm waiting for my army to go to school.

But she goes to something called the 'shop' instead.

So I go to school without her, to spy on Clara.

Very-suspicious o'clock

Clara is not at school!

This is very suspicious. Has she realised I am after her and gone into hiding? Or witness protection?

Her army isn't here either. No one is here.

Where are they?

Half past not-at-school

I find my army coming out of the 'shop' with a bag in her hand. I am about to approach her, to see if she knows where Clara is, when someone beats me to it.

It's the human known as Delphine.

Why is she talking to my army? Is she

trying to steal her away from me?

I dive behind the nearest car and listen.

'Hello, Celeste,' says Delphine.

'Hi Delphine!' says my army. 'Have you heard anything about Uncle Dylan yet?'

The Delphine human laughs. 'Oh dear me, no. It's much too soon for that.'

My army's face goes red. 'Sorry. I just thought—'

'Actually, I was hoping you'd tell me a bit more about the town,' says Delphine.

My army looks up and down the street. 'There isn't any more. You saw it all yesterday.'

'Silly me,' says Delphine. 'I meant the *outskirts* of the town. You know, who owns the farms, where Constable Hennessey lives, that sort of thing. A bit of local colour for the story I'm writing.'

Constable Hennessey? I've heard that name before. I try to remember where.

Was it— yes! It was at the school, when I was hiding in a box. According to Digby, Clara helped Constable Hennessey catch Mr Simpson.

So if I can find Constable Hennessey, he might know where she is.

I start listening again. But now my army and Delphine are talking about something completely different.

'It's just a joke,' says my army.

'What a pity,' says Delphine. 'It would have made such a good story. Well, I'd better not keep you any longer, Celeste. Thanks for the directions!'

She walks away.

I follow her.

Blue-car o'clock

Delphine gets into a blue car and drives off.

I run after it. (Ducks are very fast runners.)

Out-of-breath o'clock

Cars are faster than I thought.
  I fly after it instead.

Where-are-we-going o'clock?

The blue car drives south, towards the bend in the river where I caught and ate my first frog. It passes several humans, a couple of buildings, some trees, a house with a compost heap—

Wait, there's a single chook scratching at the compost. And she looks familiar. Is it …? Could it be …?

I fly past. Then I bank in a wide circle and fly back again, pretending to be a completely different duck.

The chook in the compost heap is definitely Clara. This must be her secret headquarters.

I fly back to my own headquarters, making dark and mysterious plans.

(They are still mysterious to me, but I'm sure that will change soon.)

Saturday
Little Dismal

To Jubilee Crystal Simpson
Somewhere on earth

Hi Jubilee, Delphine asked me about Clara today. She said she'd heard a rumour about this really clever chook, and was it a joke or wasn't it?

I was going to tell her the truth, because why should I do what Olive Hennessey says?

But then I thought, if I tell her, Olive and Clara will be really famous. And then I'll hate them more than ever.

So I told Delphine it was a joke. Ha ha.

She's so nice. We talked about names and she thinks Juliette is a cuter name than Celeste.

Love from your best friend, Juliette. (That makes us twins, right? Jubilee and Juliette!)

PS. My duck is pacing around my bedroom. She looks as if she's thinking really hard.

What do ducks think about? Eggs? Swimming? Other ducks?

I wish she could talk.

Sunday!

Half past tasty-frog

I have worked out how to tell one TODAY from the next!

I'm going to *name the days*. (I'm surprised that no one has thought of this before.)

So today is Sunday, because lying in the sun with my wings outstretched is the best position for plotting revenge.

The day after Sunday will be Mudday, because mud is full of worms and insects, and gobbling them up helps me think about revenge.

The day after Mudday will be Chooseday, because I will be busy choosing my revenge.

The day after Chooseday will be Whenday, as in, 'When will I be welcomed back into the flock and praised for my brilliant revenge?'

The day after Whenday will be Thirstday, because I have a thirst for revenge.

The day after Thirstday will be Frightday, because Clara's going to get such a fright when I take revenge on her.

The day after Frightday will be Satday, in honour of all the ducks back to the beginning of time who have sat on eggs while they plotted revenge.

The day after Satday will be—

Then we start again! The day after Satday will be Sunday, and then Mudday, and so on, for ever and ever!

I-am-brilliant o'clock

Clara could never have come up with something like this.

(Nor could Vera.)

Even-more-brilliant o'clock

I have thought of a dark and mysterious plan. And it's not dark and mysterious to me!

I wish I could tell my army about my plan. If she could understand my instructions, I would let her take part. I don't want her to feel left out.

How can I teach her to speak Duck?

Mudday

Training o'clock

This morning my army looks at me and says, 'You're going to steal my hairbrush again, aren't you?'

How did she know?

She hands me the hairbrush. 'Go on then.'

According to General Ya, a leader should always keep her followers on their toes.

So I drop the hairbrush and snatch up something else instead.

'What are you doing with my bracelet?' cries my army. 'Give it back!'

I run for the door.

I hope she's enjoying our morning training sessions as much as I am.

School o'clock

I'm going to school with my army.

I'm going to find Clara and carry out my dark and mysterious plan.

Hehehehehehehe.

But Clara isn't at school. Her army is there in the yard, but I can't see her anywhere.

I go looking for her.

I fly low and stealthy

so she will not see me.

I swoop beneath the trees,

I glide behind the houses.

I am vengeance

on silent wings—

Ahem. That was *not* a poem. That was just – random thoughts.

Or a threat! Yes, it was a threat!

Phew.

Half past definitely-not-a-poem

I find Clara at her secret headquarters, scratching in the compost heap again. There's a blue car parked a little way up the road, but I can't see any humans.

This fits in well with my plan.

I fly down the side of the house and land just before the corner. There's a large bush behind me, so no one can see me from the road and give me away.

I peep around the corner. There's the compost heap! There's Clara!

A duck less cunning than me (like Vera, for example) would probably run straight at her. But that wouldn't work. Clara would have time to prepare herself. She would pretend

Vera was a client, and then Vera wouldn't know what to do.

I would never try anything so foolish.

Instead, I will lure her to me. She'll trot around the corner of the house – and I'll attack her.

General Ya would be proud of me.

Ready-for-battle o'clock

I give my feathers a quick preen. I waggle my tail for luck. I clear my throat.

Then I say, very loudly, *'Oh my, what big, fat juicy worms there are over here! I have never seen such wonderful worms!'*

But here is the cunning part. I say it in Chook.

So basically it sounds like, 'Cluck cluck cluck, cluckety cluck cluck cluck cluck.'

(I have always been good at languages.)

Then I crouch down so Clara won't see me until the very last moment. And I say it again.

'Cluck cluck cluck, cluckety cluck cluck cluck cluck!'

This is such a brilliant plan. Clara is probably hurrying across the grass towards me at this very moment.

I urge her on with an extra 'Cluck cluck cluck!' and ready myself to leap upon her as soon as she rounds the corner...

But just as I gather my legs under me, a net falls over my head.

How-dare-they o'clock

The net tangles me and holds me and doesn't let me move. I forget about the trap I have prepared for Clara and shout in my normal voice, *'Who has attacked me? Let me at them!'*

And I begin to thrash against the net.

Somewhere above me, a human voice says, 'What? I thought it was— But it's a *duck!*'

Footsteps hurry away. I take no notice. I'm biting the net, tearing it apart, ripping it to pieces.

I get my head free, and one of my wings.

I thrash harder, until there's nothing left of the net but a small scrap wrapped around my leg.

I look up, and Clara is standing at the corner of the house, watching me with a worried expression.

It's too late to attack her. The trap is sprung, and all I can do is pretend.

'Oh, hello, Clara,' I say. *'What a surprise to see you here. I was just innocently passing by and thought this looked like a nice spot to – er – have a dustbath.'*

'Why do you have a bit of net around your leg?' she asks.

'A human dropped it on me.'

'Why?'

What a strange question. *'I doubt if there was a reason for it,'* I say. *'You know what humans are like. They're always doing idiotic things.'*

'Hmm,' says Clara. She inspects the remains of the net. *'Did you see the human?'*

'No, I was too busy with my totally innocent dustbath.'

'That's a pity,' says Clara. Then she wanders away, mumbling to herself.

At first I'm pleased, because I have fooled her. She is not the least bit suspicious.

But then I realise that this is the second time I have failed.

Great-Aunt Myrtle does not like failure.

I do not like failure.

Taking revenge on a chook should be easy.

What am I doing wrong? And how can I fix it?

Monday night
Little Dismal

To Jubilee Crystal Simpson
Somewhere on earth

Hi Jubilee, Delphine has interviewed Olive Hennessey and Digby Carella already for her article. I don't know who else. But I heard that Mrs Briggs and Mrs Fullerton are trying to get hold of her, with *their* stories about growing up in Little Dismal.

I bet they're really boring.

Anyway, I saw Delphine in the street this afternoon, and called out to her. I thought she heard me, but I guess I was wrong, because she didn't turn around. But that's okay. She's probably really busy.

Love from your best friend Juliette

PS. I wonder if Delphine knows where I live. For when she finds out about Uncle Dylan.

PPS. My duck's pacing again. Something's made her unhappy and I don't know what. I WISH she could tell me.

Chooseday

Half past yawn

I am up at first light to take my army for her training run. She's just as enthusiastic as she was on Mudday.

Breakfast o'clock

Humans keep their food in a room called 'kitchen'. I have tried to enter it several times, but my army always stops me.

Today I sneak in when she's not looking.

I'm trying to work out where they keep the frogs, when Mum-the-spy comes in.

I dive under the table and stay very quiet.

I don't want her reporting my movements back to Clara. Or Vera.

The small humans arrive, and Mum-the-spy lifts them into their chairs. My army pokes her head around the door. I think she's looking for me.

I pretend I'm not here.

'Hi Trace,' says Mum-the-spy. 'I'm running a bit late this morning. Could you give the boys their breakfast?'

'Haven't got time,' mumbles my army. 'And my name's Juliette.'

She comes in just far enough to snatch something off the table, and heads back to the door.

One of the small humans peeps under the table. 'Duck!' he squeaks.

My army spins around. 'Maybe I have got time. Max? Cody? What do you want for breakfast?'

'Duck!'

Horror-story o'clock

Sometimes, on dark winter evenings, Great-Aunt Myrtle tells the smallest ducklings the story of how Great-Grandpa Francis was eaten by a dog.

That story is a warning to all of us.

I explain to Max's bare toes that I will not be eaten.

He squeals.

'You want banana?' my army asks quickly. 'And apple?'

'Thanks, Trace,' says Mum-the-spy. 'I mean Juliette. You're a champion.'

My army mumbles something. Cody drops a piece of breakfast onto the floor.

I snap it up.

Yum. Banana-and-apple is nice.

'Bad duck!' shouts Max.

'Um – maybe I'll take them to my bedroom for breakfast,' says my army.

Mum-the-spy sounds surprised. 'Thank you,

sweetie, that would be so helpful.'

My army sweeps the small humans out of their chairs and gives them a push. 'Go and sit on my bed, okay?'

Then she checks that Mum-the-spy isn't watching, grabs me from under the table and runs out of the room.

She is very quick. I don't even have time to bite her.

The training must be having an effect.

More-breakfast o'clock

'So the duck is a secret, okay?' says my army. 'Don't tell Mum about her.'

The small humans laugh. 'Secret,' says Max.

'Duck,' says Cody.

I nibble their toes, and they share their banana-and-apple with me.

Half past why-did-I-not-know-about-banana?

My mind is sharp. My purpose is set.

Today I will get it right.

Today I *must* get it right.

I fly to school with my army. Olive is there, but Clara is not.

Good.

I fly to her secret headquarters.

Clara is at the compost heap, so I land around the far side of the house, where she can't see me.

I have decided that yesterday's plan was *too* dark and mysterious.

Today's is simpler.

For a start, there will be no clucking.

Skulking o'clock

I skulk around the yard until I find Clara's nest. I can see from the freshness of the grass that this is the one she used yesterday.

There is no egg in it. Not yet.

Hehehehehehehehehehehe.

There's a shed halfway between the compost heap and the nest. I check all around it for nets. (Today I will not be distracted by idiotic humans.)

Then I creep back to the corner of the shed.

When Clara has finished scratching, she will stroll around this corner, heading for her nest. She will not be expecting a vengeful duck.

All I have to do is wait.

Even-MORE-breakfast o'clock

There is a small pile of grain nearby. It must be part of Clara's breakfast, a snack between compost heap and nest.

But she will not want it, not after I have finished with her.

So I eat it.

Then I wait a little longer.

I'm growing impatient.

I am also growing ... sleepy.

I don't usually feel sleepy ... at this time of

morning. It must be ... because I have been thinking ... so hard.

I might just ... have a little ... lie ... down ... while I ... wait ...

Dreaming o'clock

I dream a human voice. 'Oh no,' it says. 'It's that duck again!'

Half past dreaming

'Rita. Rita, wake up. Wake up, Rita!'

Someone is shouting at me.

'Rita! You've got to wake up!'

A wing whacks me across the head, and I stumble to my feet. *'What is it? Are we under attack? Is it the pigs? Action stations! All ducklings to the rear! Prepare to charge—'*

'Rita,' says a voice close by. *'It's me, Clara.'*

I blink. Where have the pigs gone? Why do I feel so dopey? Why is Clara looking at me like that?

'You were asleep and wouldn't wake up,' she says. *'Why were you asleep?'*

It is none of her business why I was asleep. I expect I just felt like it.

In fact, I still feel like it. I might just ... lie down...

Clara pecks me. She pecks me! *'Don't fall asleep again. I have questions. Did you see a human, just before you fell asleep? Did you see a car?'* She peers into my eye. *'Did you eat anything?'*

I'm not going to tell her about the wheat. She would accuse me of stealing.

Besides, I don't want to talk to her. I don't want to talk to anyone.

This is the third time I have failed.

'Gotta go,' I mumble. *'Gotta go and do – um – duck things.'*

Then I take a quick run-up and launch myself into the air.

No, then I *try* to launch myself into the air.

But I stumble on the run-up. I trip over *my own feet* and go beak-down in the earth.

Right in front of Clara.

I finally get airborne on the fourth try.

Half past failure

I go to the river, well away from the scene of my humiliation, and nibble mournfully on a water snail.

Its shell breaks
and so does my heart.
Oh snail, so small and tasty
you will never know
the sadness
of being
a failed
duck—

A sudden flurry of wings cuts off my thoughts, and I blurt out, *'That wasn't a poem!'*

'What?' says the duck who has landed on the water in front of me.

It's my cousin Vera.

'Nothing,' I say. 'Nothing at all. Um – what are you doing here?'

'Great-Aunt Myrtle sent me to check on you,' says Vera, snatching up a snail that I was just about to eat. *'She was expecting you to have reported back by now.'*

I'm wondering whether I should confess my failure when she adds, *'I mean, how long does it take to wreak revenge on one small chook?'*

'Well,' I begin.

'Pigs are much harder than chooks,' says Vera, *'and I sorted them out in no time. You should have seen them squeal.'* She grabs another snail from under my beak. *'Mm, these aren't bad.'*

'Wait,' I say. 'You went after the pigs on the

Waddle farm? Wasn't Great-Aunt Myrtle going to do that?'

'She invited me along,' says Vera. 'Apparently she's had her eye on me for a while. Wanted to see how I'd go in a difficult situation. Do you want to hear the rude song I made up about the pigs?'

'Uh—'

'Great-Aunt Myrtle says it's brilliant. I'm going to perform it at the next Talent Night.'

Vera stops talking for long enough to scoop up the rest of the water snails. Then she shakes the mud from her beak and says, 'You didn't want any more of them, did you? Anyway, about the next Talent Night—'

I interrupt her. 'Sorry, I have to go. Got - um - things to do. Important things. Important revenge things.'

Vera tilts her head and inspects me out of one eye. 'Want some help? I mean, if you can't manage on your own—'

'Of course I can manage on my own! That's how I work best.'

'So what's the plan?' asks Vera.

But I'm already beating my wings and rising up out of the water.

As the last droplets fall from my feathers, I hear her shout, *'Do you want to see my imitation of the pigs? And how they ran? Great-Aunt Myrtle says it's hilarious.'*

Tuesday
Little Dismal

To Jubilee Crystal Simpson
Somewhere on earth

Hi Jubilee, I think I must've done something to make Delphine mad at me.

I didn't mean to. I just wanted to ask her about Uncle Dylan.

So I went to the hotel after school.

Last time I was there, your dad was the manager and we were best friends. And now I don't even know where you are.

Anyway, Mrs Thompson told me Delphine's room number. But when I knocked, Delphine flung the door open and snapped, 'What?'

She looked so angry that I forgot why I'd come. I just stood there, staring at her.

She rolled her eyes and muttered, 'This is the last thing I need.'

Then she slammed the door in my face.

Love from your friend ~~Juliette~~ Amelie

Still Chooseday

Misery o'clock

I lied to Vera. I don't have important revenge things to do. I don't have anything to do.

I'm a failure. Great-Aunt Myrtle was right to distrust me.

I should return to the pond and tell her. But how can I? She'll look right through me as if I don't exist.

And then she'll give the job to Vera.

It's such a humiliating thought that I bury my head under my wing, and pretend it is nighttime.

'Hey, duck,' whispers my army. She's lying

on her nest beside me. 'Are you unhappy too?'

Her hand strokes my feathers.

I should bite her, but I'm too miserable.

Besides, it's comforting.

'I wish you could understand me,' she whispers.

'I can,' I mumble.

'When you quack like that, it's almost like you're answering me.'

'I am answering you.'

'I wish you *were* answering me.'

I take my head out from under my wing. *'I AM ANSWERING!'*

'You know what I'd ask, if you could understand me?' she says. 'I'd get you to dance like you did the other night. To cheer us up. You know, with the wings and stuff?'

I stare at her in horror. She thought I was *dancing?* I was not *dancing,* I was showing her the ancient duck skill of unarmed combat.

How could she possibly mistake it for dancing? Dancing is not on the list!

I shrug off her hand and stand up. I raise my wings. I demonstrate the accuracy of my block, and the terrible threat of my advance and kick.

I wait for her to realise her mistake.

Instead, she gapes at me. 'You – you understood?'

'Of course I understood,' I tell her.

'But that's impossible!'

If ducks could roll their eyes, I'd do it. But we can't. So I just move my wings into a very sarcastic position.

My army leaps up and begins to pace the room. 'Maybe it was just a coincidence. Yes, that's probably it.'

'No it's not,' I say.

'I wish there was some way we could test it. Maybe if I asked you questions? And you answered one quack for yes and two quacks for no?'

'How about one quack for no and two quacks for NO,' I say.

She stares at me. 'Was that a yes or a no? I couldn't tell.'

She's kneeling on her nest now, as excited as a duckling on its first swim. 'I know! I'll ask a question, and you nod or shake your head. Like this!'

She nods, which in duck language means, 'Will you be my boyfriend?'

Why is she asking me to be her boyfriend? I'm a duck, not a drake. And besides, she's *human*.

'No,' I reply, with great dignity. *'I will not be your boyfriend. Please don't ask me again.'*

But now she's shaking her head, which means, 'I have mud on my beak.'

I look at her carefully. There's no mud.

Why are humans so strange?

Half past confusion

Things have become a little clearer. My army was not asking me to be her boyfriend.

Nor was she trying to shake mud off her beak.

It turns out humans do things differently. (I am probably the first to discover this.)

'Will you be my boyfriend?' means 'yes'. And *'I have mud on my beak'* means 'no'.

Now we've got that sorted out, she is asking questions.

'Are you and Clara friends?'

'I have mud on my beak.'

'That's good, because I hate Olive Hennessey. Does anyone else know you can understand them?'

What a ridiculous question. Every single duck in Little Dismal knows I can understand them, and so do the pigs, the cows and the chooks. I wouldn't be surprised if the magpies know, too.

But I can't say any of that. All I can do is nod.

'Will you be my boyfriend?'

'Oh,' says my army. Her head droops like a sick duckling, and I wonder if she has been forgetting to eat her dandelion greens.

But then she perks up. 'No one's said anything about it, not even Olive Hennessey. I bet they don't know really.'

Aha, when she said 'anyone else' she meant other humans.

Why do they always think it's about them?

'So, you mustn't tell anyone,' she continues. 'I'm your friend, and no one else.'

I'm beginning to wish that ducks could roll their eyes.

'Can you write, like Clara?' she asks next.

'Will you be my boyfriend?'

'Really? That's so cool! Here, write something.'

She puts a page of her memoir on the nest in front of me. She hands me a pen and I take it in my beak.

The pen breaks.

We try another one.

That one breaks, too.

(Why do all these humans have pens made by chooks? Is it some sort of business deal? Have the chooks cornered the market?)

'Maybe try not to bite it so hard?' says my army, handing me another pen.

I do writing.

Tuesday
Little Dismal

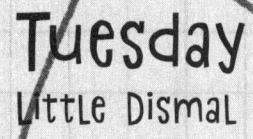
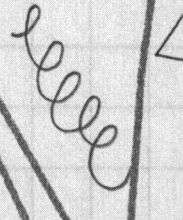

To Jubilee Crystal Simpson
Somewhere on earth

Hi Jubilee, I think I must've done something to make Delphine mad at me.

I didn't mean to. I just wanted to ask her about Uncle Dylan.

So I went to the hotel after school.

Last time I was there, your dad was the manager and we were best friends. And now I don't even know where you are.

Anyway, Mrs Thompson told me Delphine's room number. But when I knocked, Delphine

Still Chooseday

Quarter past writing

My army is very impressed with my writing. She stares at it for a long time.

Then she says, 'Um – maybe a phone would be easier. Hang on.'

She scrambles off the nest and runs out of the room. When she comes back, she's carrying a black thing. It's a bit like a squashed cockroach. A *big* squashed cockroach. Without legs.

'This is Mum's old phone,' she says. 'No sim card, so I can't use it to message Jubilee. But it's fine for a duck. Ha ha, I know that's a weird thing to say. Here.'

She puts the squashed, legless cockroach in front of me. 'That's the keypad,' she says. 'You can use your beak to tap out the letters.'

She wriggles on the nest. 'This is *so cool*. I've got my very own talking duck!'

I decide that my first message will explain that I am *not* her talking duck. She is *my* talking human.

I lower my head. I stare at the keypad. I write. 'MEHWPAJGREAGNLAE8DNKW20#M_)(OIKJUTUDFILKJL"P)F%'

Half past more-writing

'I guess a duck's beak just isn't made for typing,' says my army. She bites her lip. 'Or maybe – maybe I was wrong. Maybe you can't understand me after all.'

She's got it back to front. *I* can understand *her*, but *she* can't understand *me*.

Obviously I should have chosen an army who knew more about writing.

But I'm stuck with her for now, so when her head droops again, I hop off the nest to search for some dandelion greens.

I don't find any.

I'm searching under the nest, just in case she has hidden them, when she squeals, 'I know! Fridge letters!'

Once again, she runs out of the room. I keep looking for the dandelion greens. Even a bit of parsley would do at this stage.

My army returns with her hands full of small, colourful objects and strews them across the nest. I have never seen anything like them before. I wonder what they taste like...

'No! No, duck! Don't eat the fridge letters! They're for writing.'

I knew that.

'Now,' she says. 'Write your name. Like, Duck.' She says it again, really slowly. 'Write. Your. Name.'

I write my name.

OMYEMDAQS

Half past MORE-writing

'So you can't even spell?' she says.

What is 'spell'?

'Right,' she says. 'I'm going to teach you.'

Fridge-letters o'clock

More human mysteries. According to my army, this is a duck.

I don't believe her. It doesn't look like a duck. It doesn't walk like a duck or talk like a duck.

How can it be a duck?

Little Dismal
Wednesday

To Jubilee Crystal Simpson
Somewhere on earth

Hey Jubilee, guess what? I'm teaching my duck to spell!!!

Isn't that the weirdest thing you've ever heard? But it's true. I'm teaching her to write, too, though she keeps breaking my pens because she bites them too hard.

I'm not going to tell anyone about her, not yet. Maybe when she gets really good at spelling and writing and stuff. Maybe then.

Of course I'd tell you if you were here.

Love from your friend, Amelie

PS. Except maybe you'd laugh and call me a loser.

Thirstday

Half past egg

I am learning to write.

I could *already* write. Now I'm learning to write in human.

I have broken seven fridge letters and five pens. My army is very impressed.

Quick-hide-under-the-bed-Mum's-coming o'clock

The spy known as Mum has arrived to interrogate my army.

'Trace,' says Mum. 'I mean Juliette—'

'My name's Amelie,' says my army.

'Right. Amelie. Uh – you know that journalist, the one who's writing about growing up in small towns? Did you visit her the other day? At the hotel?'

My army sits up straight. 'Have you been spying on me?'

'No. Della Briggs told me.'

'Mrs Briggs should mind her own business.'

'Maybe,' says Mum. 'But I'm glad she told me. I don't like you hanging around with a complete stranger.'

'You make it sound as if she's some sort of criminal.'

'That's not what I meant—'

'And anyway, she's not a stranger. She came and spoke to our class.'

'Yes, but—'

'And I *asked* you if it was all right to talk to her, and you said yes. It's not my fault if you've forgotten.'

Mum sighs. 'Trace—'

'Don't call me that!'

'Sorry, I mean Juliette – I mean Amelie.'

That's where I stop listening. Because my army has given me an idea.

An *excellent* idea.

Tomorrow morning I'll let her run around the backyard *fifteen* times, as a special treat.

Frightday

Half past egg

We are having breakfast on the nest again.

Today it's something called weetbix.

'Where is the banana?' I ask.

I search Max.

I search Cody.

I search my army.

Why are they giggling? Breakfast is a serious matter.

Window o'clock

My army tells me that glass is also called 'window'.

She's going to leave her window open, so I can fly in and out whenever I like.

She is a good army. I decide to keep her, despite the lack of banana.

Excellent-idea o'clock

This morning I do not try to hide from Clara. This morning I fly several circles over her compost heap, then swoop down and land next to a particularly tasty clump of grass.

I begin to eat, watching Clara out of the corner of my eye.

She is snapping up the worms and the earwigs, but not the snails. (Chooks have *no idea* about fine dining.)

Gradually I edge closer, until I am within range of the snails.

Yum. Crunchy.

Clara turns and looks at me. *'I was going to come and find you. I have a footprint I want you to see.'*

She trots away, and I follow her, taking several snails with me.

We stop at a patch of earth where a human has trodden.

'This footprint,' says Clara, *'does not belong to Constable Dad, Olive or Digby. I have checked their shoes, just as Inspector Garcia checked all the shoes in Episode 13 of* Death in the City.*'*

What is she talking about? Why this sudden obsession with shoes?

'So,' she says, *'have you seen this footprint before?'*

I pretend to study it. *'No.'*

'Are you sure you didn't see any humans when you were caught in the net? Or before you fell asleep? Were there any cars nearby?'

Is she trying to embarrass me? I don't want to talk about the net, or about falling asleep. They were both very small mistakes, and I have moved on from them.

I'm about to say so, when I remember my new plan. So instead of snapping at her, I say, *'Sorry. I didn't see anyone.'*

(I'm not really sorry. This is *subterfuge* or trickery. Like spying, it is on the list under revenge, warfare and general thuggery.)

Clara peers at me out of one eye. I gulp a snail, trying to look as innocent as possible. (To Clara, not to the snails. It's no use trying to look innocent to snails; they have a suspicious nature.)

My subterfuge seems to work. Clara goes back to the earwigs and we eat side-by-side, almost as if we are friends.

Hehehehehehe.

After a while, I say casually, *'Don't know if you can help me or not—'*

'I told you, no revenge cases,' says Clara.

'This isn't a revenge case. I'm just looking

for advice. There's a new sheep stealer in town, and I was wondering—'

Clara's head jerks up. An earwig tumbles from her beak and scurries for cover. *'What? Who? Where?'*

'Her name's Delphine.'

'Whose sheep has she stolen?' demands Clara.

'Er – no one's. Not yet. But she's definitely going to.'

'How do you know? Where's your evidence?'

'Evidence?' I say. *'What is evidence?'*

'Where are the clues?' says Clara, still staring at me. *'What has she done?'*

'Done? Why must she have done something?'

Clara ruffles her feathers in annoyance. *'You're wasting my time. I have more important things to think about. Come back when you have evidence.'*

And she stalks away.

Half past Clara

I don't understand. I thought she would leap at the chance to catch another sheep stealer.

I thought she would rush into town and arrest Delphine, and that would get her into trouble, because Delphine is *not really a sheep stealer*.

(This is also subterfuge.)

And then everyone would laugh at Clara for making a fool of herself, instead of laughing at ducks.

It was a brilliant plan. Why does she have to spoil it by needing evidence?

Friday night
Little Dismal

To Jubilee Crystal Simpson
Somewhere on earth

Hi Jubilee, want to hear something weird? Mrs Savage gave me a poem.

She slipped it into my hand when she was giving out worksheets, as if it was some kind of secret between us.

Anyway, it's called 'Kindness', and it's by a lady called Naomi Shihab Nye. It's about losing things, and being on a bus that never stops, and someone dead by the side of the road. Yeah, weird stuff like that.

I'd ask Mum what it means, but she's too busy.

Love from your best friend ~~Amelie~~ Marguerite

PS. Delphine tried to talk to me after school today. But I don't want to talk to her, not after she was so horrible to me.

PPS. I think my duck's name is Rado. Or Ratso. Something like that. She is so cute!

Satday

Thinking o'clock

I have spent the day thinking about clues. Clara will not arrest Delphine without evidence that she is a sheep stealer.

But Delphine is *not* a sheep stealer. So there is no evidence.

Another-excellent-idea o'clock!

I'm practising my writing as hard as I can.

Already I can write my name. Soon I will be able to do more. *Much* more.

Hehehehehehehehehehe.

HOMEWORK SHEET – MATHS

~~Tracy Lawless~~
MARGUERITE

1. Work out 0.7 + 0.9
2. Write the Roman numeral XXXVIII in figures
3. I have $15. I spend $2.50. How much have I got left?
4. A piece of wood measuring 4 m is cut into eight equal lengths. How long will each bit be?
5. What is 28 multiplied by 103?
6. Write down a multiple of 7 between 40 and 50.
7. Evie's and Dylan's ages add up to 19. Evie is 3 years older than Dylan. How old are they?
8. $\frac{2}{3} + \frac{1}{6} =$
9. There is a 50% discount on an item that costs $200. What is the new cost of the item?
10. Add 15 minutes to 1:05 PM.

Monday
Little Dismal

To Jubilee Crystal Simpson
Somewhere on earth

Hi Jubilee, I took my duck for a ride on my bike after school, out to the tip. (Her name's Rita, not Ratso, and she loves riding in the basket.)

We were on our way back through town when Delphine drove up beside us in her blue Toyota. She wound her window down and said, all nice and sweet, 'Hi Juliette, I've been looking everywhere for you. Can I have a word?'

I kept riding.

She followed alongside, saying, 'I really need to talk to you.'

I sped up. She sped up too, until we were racing towards the hotel.

But then suddenly I thought, what if she's heard back from the Innocence Project? What if she wants to talk to me about Uncle Dylan?

I braked so hard that Rita nearly fell out of the basket. 'Sorry, Rita,' I whispered. 'But this is important.'

She hopped down and started hunting for something in the gutter, while I waited for Delphine to reverse back.

'Is it about Uncle Dylan?' I asked her.

But Delphine was staring at Rita. 'Is that your duck?'

She sounded angry, though I don't know why. It's not as if she'd ever seen Rita before.

'Is it about Uncle Dylan?' I asked her again.

She turned back to me, and for a moment she looked kind of blank. 'Uncle...'

But I guess she was just distracted. Because then she smiled and said, 'Yes, of *course* it's about Uncle Dylan. And it's excellent news. I've heard back from the people at the Innocence Project, and they're sure he didn't do what he was accused of. They can't prove it yet, but they will.'

I wish I could tell Dad. But Delphine said I mustn't breathe a word to anyone, because if I did it'd mess everything up and then Uncle Dylan would never get out of jail.

I don't understand how that could happen if he's innocent. But I guess Delphine knows more about these things than I do.

Anyway, then she said, 'I owe you an apology, Juliette. The other day – I was under a lot of stress, but I shouldn't have snapped at you like that.'

'It's okay,' I said. 'But I'm not Juliette anymore. I'm Marguerite.'

'A beautiful name,' said Delphine. 'Now, there's something I need your help with—'

But before she could tell me what it was, Mrs Briggs and Mrs Fullerton turned up.

'Yoohoo, Delphine!' called Mrs Fullerton. 'We've been chasing you all over town.'

'And now we have you at last,' said Mrs Briggs, shoving me out of the way and leaning in the car window. She beamed at Delphine. 'It's all very well talking to the youngsters, like Tracy here, about growing up in a country town, but if you want the *really* interesting stories—'

'—then you need to talk to us,' said Mrs Fullerton.

'And our friends,' said Mrs Briggs. She whipped a piece of paper out from behind her back. 'So we've drawn up a roster for you.'

Delphine was looking a bit stunned. (Everyone looks a bit stunned when Mrs Fullerton and Mrs Briggs get hold of them.) 'Er – I don't really need—'

'Of course you do,' said Mrs Fullerton, trotting around to the other side of the car and climbing into the passenger seat. 'No one knows this town like we do. So, let's see, we've got you booked in with Della here for the next couple of hours. Then me.'

'You won't believe some of the things we have to tell you,' said Mrs Briggs.

'Then first thing tomorrow morning,' said Mrs Fullerton, 'you're talking to Damien Potter—'

'We'll go with you,' added Mrs Briggs, 'because some of his stories might be a little unreliable.'

'After Damien, we'll go to Daphne Talbot. We went to school with her, didn't we, Della? She is an absolute scream.'

'Do you have a little tape recorder?' asked Mrs Briggs, getting into the back seat. 'Or do you take notes? This is so interesting, isn't it? Now where shall we do the first interview, I wonder?'

'Let's go to my place,' said Mrs Fullerton. 'Turn left at the next corner, Delphine, and we'll direct you from there.'

And they drove away.

Love from your friend Marguerite

PS. I don't think Delphine was happy about being kidnapped. But it was actually kind of funny.

Chooseday

Half past egg

I have practised the message I need to write over and over again, until it is perfect. Now it is time to find Clara.

But first I take my army for her early morning run around the garden.

'I hate you,' she says, as we go around for the eighth time. But she smiles as she says it.

Half past training

After our run, I explain that tomorrow we will have unarmed combat lessons.

UNOMD KOMBOT

She stares at my fridge-letter message. 'What?'

It seems perfectly clear to me. I poke the message with my foot, to show her how important it is.

She screws up her face. 'Is that word supposed to be "gumboot"?'

I am shaking mud off my beak.

'Or – kombot, is that like some sort of robot?'

I am shaking mud off my beak.

'Nom, is that like food? You know, how the twins say nom nom?'

I am shaking mud off my beak.

'Um – romcom? Like a romantic comedy? Only for robots?'

I am shaking—

No, I give up in disgust. Why can't humans spell?

Sheep o'clock

It's not hard to find a sheep in Little Dismal. There are far too many of them.

Plus they are very bad-tempered when you try to pull their wool out. Even when it's for a good cause.

But in the end I manage to get a good hank of wool in my beak. And I set off to find Clara.

Where-is-she o'clock?

She is not at her secret headquarters.

She is not at the school.

She is not at the river or anywhere on the main street of Little Dismal.

At last I track her down to the back door of the McAllister farmhouse, where she is picking through a pile of shoes.

I go into stealth mode. I cruise past the house on hushed wings, being very careful not to quack with excitement. That would give me away. And I would drop the wool, and the note.

I land at the front of the farmhouse, and run down the side. When I peep around the corner, Clara is measuring the bottom of a boot with her claw, completely unaware that she is being spied on.

Hehehehehehehehehe.

I wait until she has returned the boot to the pile and is busy choosing another one. Then I dash forward, drop the note and the hank of wool behind her, and race back into hiding.

She doesn't see the note straight away. She measures each shoe, and inspects it carefully, while I grow more and more impatient.

But at last she has finished. She turns away from the house – and sees the note and the wool.

Her head bobs in surprise. She arches her neck. She steps forward cautiously.

She inspects the wool first, checking it from every direction.

Then she reads the note I have placed beside it.

To my surprise, she doesn't race off to arrest Delphine (and make a fool of herself, etc etc). Instead, she reads the note again. She peers at it from different angles.

She stands there and thinks about it.

This is ridiculous. She's supposed to be a detective. Why isn't she doing detective stuff?

I decide to give her some help.

I wander around the corner in a casual sort of way, as if I was looking for something. *'I'm sure there was a pond around here somewhere,'* I murmur to myself. *'Alas, someone must have moved it.'*

I'm pretending that I haven't yet seen Clara.

(More subterfuge.)

But when I'm close to her, I give a start. *'Clara, is that you? I didn't see you there. Oh, I am so astonished.'*

(I am an excellent actor.)

I pretend to see the note and the wool for the first time. *'What is that? Gosh, it looks like evidence!'*

Clara squints at me. *'Rita, did you leave this here?'*

'Me? Of course it wasn't me. Look at the note. It says "stolen by Delphine".'

'Hm,' says Clara.

But still she does not race off to arrest Delphine.

I will have to be even more cunning.

'You asked me about a car,' I say thoughtfully. *'I did see one parked near your house, on the day some idiotic human dropped a net over my head. But I had forgotten about it.'*

Clara's eyes brighten. *'What sort of car?'*

'The sort with wheels. I believe it also had windows.'

'No, no, no, what breed of car?'

I stare at her in surprise. *'Do cars have breeds? Well then, let me think. I doubt if it was a Muscovy. Or an Indian runner. Completely the wrong colour. And the wrong shape. In fact, I can't think of a breed that looks at all like—'*

'Never mind,' says Clara. *'What colour was it?'*

'It was blue,' I tell her.

(Was it blue? I can't remember. But who *does* have a blue car? Delphine!)

Hehehehehehehehehehe.

Whenday

Half past morning-run

I'm sitting on the nest next to my army when Mum-the-spy puts her head around the door.

It is too late to hide.

'Tracy?' she says. 'I mean Amelie? I was wondering if— Uh, where did the duck come from?'

'She's mine,' mumbles my army.

Mum blinks. 'The twins kept saying "duck", and I thought they were dreaming. Has she got a name?'

'Rita.' My army sits up. 'I'm not getting rid of her.'

'I didn't say anything about getting rid of her,' says Mum. 'Would she like some breakfast, do you think?'

I hop down from the nest and march across to her. *'What do you have? Worms? Frog's eggs? Grasshoppers?'*

'She's very talkative, isn't she,' says Mum, peering down at me. 'I wonder what she's saying.'

'Nothing,' my army says quickly. 'She's not saying anything.' She slides off the nest and picks me up.

I don't approve of being picked up without permission, so I bite her nose.

My army puts me down again, glares at Mum, and says, 'That means she likes me.'

'I'm sure it does,' says Mum. 'Would you both like some breakfast? By some miracle, the twins are still asleep, so we might actually get a chance to talk for a change.'

'I get first choice of grasshoppers,' I tell her.

There-are-no-grasshoppers o'clock

My army eats something called toast-and-jam, but Mum says it's not good for ducks.

She might be wrong, so I fly up onto the table to try it out. My army squawks. Mum snatches the toast-and-jam away before I can eat it.

She is very quick. I wonder if she'd be interested in leaving whoever she is spying for and joining my army instead. Perhaps I will write a note later, offering her the job.

But for now she gives me something called cracked corn, which is not as nice as grasshoppers or frog's eggs.

I eat it quickly and head off to find Clara.

Half past cracked-corn

Once again, I have trouble tracking her down. But on my third circuit of the town and surrounding farms I spot her running and flapping and fluttering down the street after a blue car.

Luckily for Clara, the car does not go far. It stops in front of a house, and three humans go inside.

One of them is Delphine.

I wait until Clara has caught up with the car and is crouching behind it, watching the house. Then I swoop down and land beside her.

'*Hi, Clara,*' I say, as if I have arrived entirely by accident.

'*Shhhh!*' she hisses, and she seizes my wing in her beak and hauls me behind the back wheel.

War has been declared for less. General Ya once laid waste to an entire farm after a cow accidentally stood on her foot.

But I am playing a longer game.

So instead of shouting, attacking, or calling in reinforcements, I peer down my beak and say, *'Please do not disrespect my feathers like that.'*

'I'm on a stake-out,' whispers Clara. *'I don't*

want Delphine to know that anyone is watching her.'

This is the best news yet. But I don't flap my wings and quack with delight. I say, as if I have no interest at all in the answer, *'Why are you watching Delphine?'*

Without taking her eyes off the house, Clara says, *'Take a look at this car. Is it the one you saw on the day of the net incident?'*

I pretend to study the car. *'Hmm,'* I say. *'It certainly looks the same. Not that I am an expert—'*

Clara interrupts me. *'I have checked the tyre prints, and found similar ones just down the road from my place. Just as Inspector Garcia found the tyre prints of Half-Tongue Harry's car around the corner from the bank. So I'm watching Delphine to see what she's up to. Why did she try to trap me—'*

Now it's my turn to interrupt. *'Someone tried to trap you?'*

'The net, the drugged wheat. What else could it be?'

Chooks! They are as bad as humans; they always think it's about them.

'What about the sheep stealing?' I ask her. *'The evidence—'*

'I don't trust that evidence,' says Clara. *'Now go away, before Delphine sees you and grows suspicious.'*

Wednesday night
Little Dismal

To Jubilee Crystal Simpson
Somewhere on earth

Hi Jubilee, I had breakfast with Mum this morning. Yeah, that was a surprise! It was kind of nice, actually.

I didn't mean to say anything about Uncle Dylan. But the words came out before I could stop them.

'Do you ever think that maybe Uncle Dylan didn't do what Constable Hennessey said he did?'

Mum looked startled. 'Who've you been talking to?'

'No one. I just thought—'

'Listen, Trace,' said Mum, 'Sorry – is it Amelie now? I can't keep up. Anyway, I know you liked Dylan. He could be real charming when he put his mind to it. But you never saw the other side of him, and I'm glad of it. He's a nasty piece of work.'

Maybe I should have told her about the Innocence Project. Maybe that would have changed her mind.

Except I couldn't. Because I promised.

Anyway, this afternoon Mum picked me up from school and we went to the airport to get my stepdad Laurie. I wasn't going to go, but Mum said he'd be disappointed if I wasn't there.

So in the end I went, even though the twins were being even more annoying than usual. On the way home, they kept saying 'duck duck duck', so Mum told Laurie about Rita.

But I guess that was all right, because she said Rita was cute, and didn't say anything about getting rid of her. And Laurie said he used to have a pet duck called Dolores, and he couldn't wait to meet Rita.

But then something weird happened. We were driving past the police station when Olive and Constable Hennessey came out the door together. And Olive looked so happy.

Actually, they both looked happy.

And I was thinking about how, when we were little, I used to go to Olive's place to play Barbies. Her mum was alive back then and made all these cute uniforms for them.

Only then Constable Hennessey arrested Uncle Dylan, and Dad said I wasn't allowed to play with Olive anymore.

And then Mum and Dad split up.

And then you came, and Olive was horrible to us.

Only she wasn't, was she? It was the other way round.

We were horrible to her.

And I can't remember who started it, you or me.

Love from Marguerite

Thirstday

Training o'clock

I take my army for her early morning run around the yard.

To my surprise, the human male called Laurie steps out of the house, yawns, stretches, and joins us.

'I didn't know you were into running, Trace,' he says, as we turn into the third lap.

'I'm not,' she says. 'But Rita keeps stealing my things.'

Laurie nods. 'That sounds about right. It's exactly the sort of thing Dolores would have done.'

I have never heard of a duck called Dolores. But it is a very fine name. Almost as good as Rita.

We reach the back doorstep and I put the bracelet down. My army snatches it up and says, 'Just stop stealing my stuff, okay?'

Laurie laughs and says, 'I don't know, it's not a bad way to start the day.' Then he looks at the ground. 'Trace, I know you and I don't always get on—'

'I'm not going to call you Dad,' says my army.

'I don't want you to. You've already got a dad.' He looks up. 'It's just – I've been running a bit while I'm away. Maybe we could go for a run together in the mornings. Only if you want to…'

My army shrugs, as if she's settling her wings. 'Maybe. Okay.'

Half past training

As soon as my army leaves for school,

Mum sits on the back step next to Laurie. (At least, I thought his name was Laurie. But I was wrong. It is Sweetheart.)

They talk about my army.

'I've been so worried about her, Sweetheart,' she says. 'I just wish she hadn't taken up with Jubilee Simpson. That girl was mean, and maybe she had good reason for it, but that doesn't help Tracy. She's like her dad, a bit too easily influenced.'

Sweetheart puts his arm around her, and she rests her head on his shoulder and says, 'But she seems a lot happier since she got Rita...'

Of course she's happier. A duck always improves matters.

I wander over to Max and Cody, who are playing in the earth. They are very pleased to see me.

'Duck!' they scream.

'Rita!'

I wonder if they would be interested in an unarmed combat lesson.

First, I make sure they are watching closely. This is not hard. I don't even have to nip their toes.

Because they are so keen, I decide to skip the part about distance and positioning, and come back to it later.

For now, I go straight into block pivot kick.

'Did you get that?' I ask them.

The answer is yes, though they don't say so. Instead, they scramble to their feet and copy me.

They get it wrong, of course, but this is only a first lesson.

So I show them again, more slowly, explaining as I go. *'Your enemy is coming at you,'* I say. *'You raise your wing to block their attack. Then pivot, like this—'*

Max falls over, but immediately scrambles back to his feet. I give him another chance.

'Pivot like this – then kick their legs from under them, and bite them!'

They particularly like the last bit.

As for me, I'm impressed. Their movements are not perfect, but they're off to a good start. And most importantly, they are enthusiastic.

Perhaps I should have chosen them as my army, right from the beginning, instead of Tracy.

I turn back to Cody and Max. *'Right, we're going to run through that again. And this time we will include a double block before the pivot. Are you ready?'*

We're working our way up to the double block when a voice behind me says, 'Oh look, Sweetheart, Rita's dancing. And the boys are copying her!'

I sigh. I am *not* dancing. It's not on the list, so of course I'm not dancing.

I turn around, determined to explain.

But I have barely started when Mum puts

her hand over her mouth and says, 'Oh no. Tracy's dancing lessons. I promised her, weeks ago – and then I forgot all about them!'

Half past definitely-not-dancing

I try to take my new army with me when I go to check on Clara. They are keen, but Mum will not let them.

Apparently they must do something called 'nap' instead.

I try to explain to Mum that it will be good experience for them, and that if they are lucky I might even let them bite Clara.

She shoos me out the door, and Sweetheart shuts it in my face.

'You're robbing your children of a valuable opportunity,' I shout.

No answer.

These people have no idea how to be good parents.

Why-won't-anyone-do-what-I tell-them o'clock?

Clara is still staking out Delphine. I suggest several times that she skip straight to the arrest, but she takes no notice.

I'll have to think of some way of hurrying her along.

Friday
Little Dismal

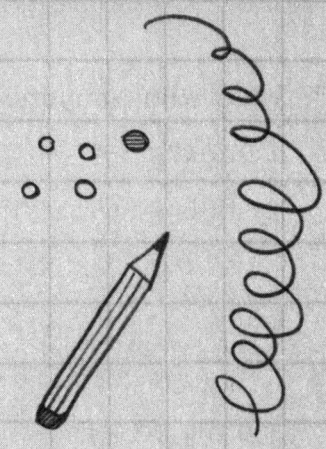

To Jubilee Crystal Simpson
Somewhere on earth

Hey Jubilee, guess what???? I'm starting dancing lessons next term!!!! In Yabby Creek!

Mum arranged it while I was at school. She explained how Rita was dancing with the twins yesterday, and that's what reminded her. And as a thank you to Rita, she bought some more fridge letters, because she'd seen her playing with them.

I didn't tell her about Rita learning to spell. But I *did* show her the kindness poem. She must've read it through about a hundred times, because she didn't say anything for ages. And then I realised she was crying.

She used to cry a lot. But not since she met Laurie.

Anyway, she said the poem was beautiful, and the person who wrote it must know heaps about the world and how sad it could be, and how sometimes kindness was the only thing that got you through it.

Then she said she was sorry she'd forgotten about the dancing lessons, and *really* sorry she hadn't had much time for me lately, and she was determined to do better.

So that started me crying. And Laurie gave us both a hug. I think you were wrong about him. He's not so bad.

from your friend Marguerite

PS. Mum said you can practise kindness.

Like practising swimming and stuff. And the more you do it, the better you get at it. So I'm going to make a little bag for the new fridge letters so Rita can carry them around her neck.

I hope she likes it.

PPS. I've been thinking about how mean we were to Olive Hennessey. You definitely started it. I remember now.

But I'm pretty sure Mum would say that was no excuse. I'm pretty sure she'd say I didn't have to follow you. I didn't have to hide things in Olive's schoolbag and pretend she'd stolen them. I didn't have to lie about her.

Mum'd be so ashamed of me if she knew. So would Laurie.

I don't want them to be ashamed of me. I don't want to be ashamed of myself.

But I am.

I think I have to do something to make it better. But I don't know what.

Satday

Gift o'clock

My army has given me my own fridge letters. In a bag.

It is a gift.

Ducks do not give gifts. They are not on the list.

But I'm going to keep the letters anyway. (Except for the Q and the Z. I can see no use for them, so I have eaten them.)

I've also decided to keep my army. I'll have to tell Max and Cody that their services are no longer needed.

Or perhaps...

A shiver of excitement runs through me.

Perhaps I'll keep all three of them. I will have a *bigger* army!

Sunday

Still-thinking o'clock
Still thinking about how I can speed up Clara's investigation.

Half past still-thinking
Still thinking.

Half past STILL-still-thinking
I have eaten the X as well. Hopefully it will inspire me.

Monday
Little Dismal

To Jubilee Crystal Simpson
Somewhere on earth

Hi Jubilee, today I apologised to Olive Hennessey.

It's the hardest thing I've ever done. My mouth was dry and my voice was shaking and I thought I was going to be sick. And it probably wasn't a very good apology because the words kept getting stuck in my throat, and later I thought of a whole lot of things I should have said but didn't.

When I was done, Olive just nodded and said, 'Okay.' Then she walked away.

I guess I don't deserve anything more than that.

I was still shaky for a while afterwards. But then I felt sort of emptier. In a good way.

Does that make sense?

I guess everyone still hates me. Except for Mum and Laurie and the twins. And Rita. And maybe Mrs Savage. If you were here, you'd probably say I should hate them back.

But I'm trying not to.

From ~~Marguerite~~ Tracy

PS. Mrs Savage asked me if I'd play footy next term, and I said yes.

Chooseday

Half past egg

While Sweetheart and First Army go on their morning run, I do training with Second and Third Army, a.k.a. Max and Cody.

They are coming along well with their blocks and pivots, but still have a tendency to fall over on the kicks.

When First Army gets back from her run, she joins in. So does Sweetheart.

Mum watches us and laughs.

Why is this funny? Doesn't she understand what I am doing for her children? I hope she won't mind too much when I take them away.

But for now, I go looking for Clara.

I have decided that I will be honest with her.

(Not really. I have decided that I will *pretend* to be honest with her.)

So today there will be no stealth. I will be completely straightforward.

Just as soon as I have planted the evidence.

Completely-straightforward o'clock

I find Clara at the Favretto farm, hiding around the corner of the tractor shed. I circle down and land beside her, making sure I'm not visible from the farmhouse.

'Hi Clara,' I say. *'Still staking out Delphine?'*

'I have worked out why she was trying to trap me,' she whispers. *'It was an attempt to get Little Dismal's best detective out of the way. But you foiled her plans by falling into the traps yourself.'*

'I did?'

'You did. Well done, Rita!'

No one has said *'Well done, Rita'* in ages. For a moment, I am overcome. Perhaps I should tell Clara the truth…

But then she says, *'Now, the first trap was set on a Monday two weeks ago, and the second on a Tuesday. There has been nothing since then—'*

What? She's using the names of my days! But I have told no one about them. How did she discover them?

And why is she saying one of them wrong?

'It's not Monday,' I tell her. *'It's Mudday.'*

Clara stares at me. *'What are you talking about?'*

So I explain how I named the days, and how I use them in my diary. I could accuse her of stealing them, but I don't. Instead, I very generously offer to let her use them in her own diary.

'But the days already have names,' she says. *'Everyone uses them. Everyone except ducks.'*

She's wrong. She must be wrong. She's trying to claim my invention for herself.

I will not tell her the truth after all.

'So why does Delphine want me out of the way?' she continues. *'Is she a criminal planning a bank heist? Or, since there is no bank in Little Dismal, a post-office-and-grocery-store heist?'*

'Listen,' I say, remembering my plan, 'I'm sorry about that note.'

Clara's head jerks up. *'You admit that you wrote it?'*

'Of course I wrote it. But I should have known it was the wrong way to go about it.'

She peers at me out of one eye. *'The wrong way to go about what?'*

'I'm worried about my human,' I say.

'I didn't know you had a human.'

'Her name is Tracy.'

Clara blinks. *'She is not a nice human. Why did you choose her?'*

I wasn't expecting that question. So I ignore it and continue with my plan.

'Whenever she spends time with Delphine,' I say, *'she comes home with strange ideas. Delphine may be stealing sheep; she may not. But I fear she's not who she pretends to be.'*

'Why didn't you tell me this before?'

'You wanted evidence,' I remind her. *'And I have no evidence. Perhaps I'm wrong.'* (I know this will convince her. We ducks never admit that we are wrong.) *'Perhaps Delphine is completely innocent. But I must look out for my human.'*

'You must,' says Clara. She is no longer suspicious. Now she's looking interested…

Half past subterfuge

Which is how we come to fly in the window of Delphine's hotel room.

Clara will search while I keep watch.

Hehehehehehehehehe.

Keeping-watch o'clock

Clara is looking in all the wrong places. Who cares about Delphine's suitcase? Who cares about the shoes in the wardrobe?

Should I give a hint? Should I nudge Clara towards the pillow where I planted the evidence?

I open my beak to make a casual suggestion – but Clara beats me to it. *'Hmm,'* she squawks from the depths of the wardrobe. *'This is interesting.'*

'What is it?' I ask her.

'Her shoes are the right size,' says Clara. *'But the one that left the footprint isn't here. There is also a book.'*

I don't care about shoes and a book. Why is she wasting time? I want her to find—

'A book of poems,' says Clara.

I tumble off the windowsill and stick my head in the wardrobe. *'Poems? What sort of poems?'*

'This one,' says Clara, *'is about feathers—'*

I snatch the book away from her and drag it out into the middle of the room.

I stare at the name of the poet.

I spell it out slowly, the way Tracy taught me.
E-M-I-L-Y

Clara is trying to get the book back, but I won't let go of it. In the end she gives up and returns to the wardrobe.

I'm still trying to work out the rest of the name. The letters swim before my eyes. Surely I'm imagining things.

EMILY D-U-C-K-I-N-S-O-N

My legs are shaking. My heart is beating so hard that I'm sure the aunties can hear it from their pond.

These poems were written by a duck!

But how is that possible?

What about the list?

Meanwhile, Clara has finished with the wardrobe and is poking around on the nest-side table. She gives a little squawk. *'A letter! What does it say...'*

I open the book and riffle through the pages with my beak. There are So. Many. Poems.

I find the one about feathers. But I'm too excited to read more than the first couple of words.

'Clara,' I say. *'Could you read this poem to me?'*

'Just a minute,' she says, with her eye hovering over the letter.

I don't know what a minute is, but it's far too long.

'Clara, I need you to read this poem.'

'Yes, yes... hmm... signed by Eddie Smythe... seems perfectly innocent ... but why has

someone written ED7 in the bottom corner? I wonder ... could it be a code?'

'CLARA, I NEED YOU TO READ THIS POEM!'

'Shhhh! Not so loud!' She cocks her head and listens, then hops down from the little table with the letter in her beak. 'What's this about a poem?'

'This one.' I tap it with my foot.

Clara drops the letter and reads:

'Hope is the thing with feathers
That perches in the soul,
And sings the tune without the words,
And never stops at all.'

It's the most beautiful thing I have ever heard. 'Read it again,' I whisper.

She reads it again. 'That is a very nice poem,' she says.

'And it was written by a duck!'

'Are you sure? Let me see. The poet is Emily D—'

She breaks off at the sound of footsteps outside the door. Someone is coming.

Clara drags the book of poems into the wardrobe, backs out and throws herself against the wardrobe door until it shuts.

Then she snatches up the letter and we both flutter onto the windowsill, and down to the ground below.

The door of Delphine's room opens and closes.

I hear her gasp. 'Someone's been here.'

Clara and I press ourselves against the wall of the hotel, in case she looks out the window.

'My letter,' whispers Delphine. 'My letter's gone.'

Wednesday
Little Dismal

To Jubilee Crystal Simpson
Somewhere on earth

Dear Jubilee, things have just got really weird. And I don't know what to think.

Delphine must have escaped from Mrs Briggs and Mrs Fullerton at last, because she was waiting for me after school today.

When she saw me, she wound down her car window. 'Were you in my hotel room yesterday?' she asked.

I propped my bike against the fence. 'No.'

'So you didn't leave this on my bed?' She held

up a bit of paper.

I guess it was a map, though it was really rough, as if a little kid had drawn it.

'I've never seen it before,' I told her.

'Okay,' she said. 'I didn't think it was you, but I had to ask.'

She slumped back against the car seat and rubbed her eyes. Then she looked at me really hard, as if she was trying to see right inside me. 'Can you keep a secret, Marguerite?'

I didn't tell her I wasn't Marguerite anymore. 'I won't say anything about Uncle Dylan.'

She shook her head. 'It's a far bigger secret than Uncle Dylan. A really big, important secret.'

So of course I said, 'Yes!'

'Are you sure?' she said. 'Because if you tell anyone about this, some very bad people are going to go free. And the good people will get punished.'

I had to cross my heart and hope to die three times before she believed me. Then she looked around to make sure there was no one nearby, lowered her voice and said, 'I've been lying to you.'

What???

'I'm not really a journalist,' she said. 'I'm a federal police officer, and I'm here undercover.'

By this time my mouth was hanging open.

'I can't tell you any more,' she said. 'I wasn't even supposed to tell you that much, but I think you'd already guessed it. You're a smart kid, Marguerite.'

I *hadn't* already guessed it. I hadn't guessed anything like it! But I didn't tell her that, because I kind of wanted her to go on thinking I was a smart kid.

In the end, she told me one other thing.

It knocked all the breath out of me. 'You're investigating *Constable Hennessey?*'

'Oops,' said Delphine, 'that just slipped out.'

'Why are you investigating him?'

'Forget I said it, okay? But now you know the truth. And here's the thing, it looks as if someone is trying to interfere with my investigation. So I'm going to have to bring it forward, and I need your help. Are you willing to play your part?'

A couple of weeks ago I would've said yes straight off. But today, something stopped me.

'I – I'll have to ask Mum,' I said.

Delphine shook her head. 'This is too important to bring anyone else into it. I'm trusting you, Marguerite. The success or failure of my investigation is in your hands.'

What do you do when a federal police officer says something like that to you? You kind of have to say yes, don't you? It's probably illegal not to.

So that's what I did.

From Tracy

PS. I keep thinking of Olive's happy face when she was with her dad. I want to tell her about

Delphine's investigation. I want to tell Mum, too, and ask her advice.

But I can't, because I *promised*.

Thirstday

Half past meeting-up-with-Clara

'Do chooks have a list?' I ask casually.

We're down by the river, which is a good place to think. We flew here – or rather, I flew and Clara hopped and fluttered and bumbled and took three times as long.

But I didn't laugh at her. Because she liked the poem that was written by a duck. And she read it to me. Twice.

'What sort of list?' she asks, without looking up from Delphine's letter. *'A list of things we like to eat? Of course.'*

'No, a list of things you can and can't do.'

'You mean the rules of the chookyard?'

'Maybe,' I say. 'What are these rules?'

'*1. Get up Early So You Don't Miss Out,*' recites Clara. '*2. Keep A Clean House So As Not To Attract Rats. 3. A Varied Diet Is A Healthy Diet.*'

That's not a list. That's just sensible advice. Even Great-Aunt Myrtle could not disagree with it.

'*So you don't have a list like—*' I try to imagine what sort of things might be on a chook's list. '*Clucking, panicking, running away from ducks, being a detective?*'

Clara looks up at last. *'If there was such a list, "being a detective" wouldn't be on it. I'm the first chook to ever do such a thing.'*

She goes back to studying the letter. But all I can think of is the fact that she is the first chook to be a detective. Ever.

Just as I'm the first duck to be a poet.

Except I'm not. Emily Duckinson waddled this path before me. And she has been published. In a book!

Perhaps Great-Aunt Myrtle was wrong...

'I'm sure this is in code,' says Clara. *'And ED7 is the key. But what does it mean?'*

I want to tell her that there is no code. And that if she keeps going with this investigation, she will make an even greater fool of herself than I had intended.

Because according to Tracy, Delphine is not a journalist after all.

She's a police officer.

Except – that's what I want, isn't it? I

want Clara to make a fool of herself, so that everyone will laugh at her instead of ducks. And Great-Aunt Myrtle will welcome me back to the pond with great honour.

But Great-Aunt Myrtle won't read poems to me. She won't say that a poem is nice.

'Clara,' I begin.

She interrupts me. *'The book of poems. The poet's initials were ED! And wasn't the nice poem on page 7? Rita, can you remember that page?'*

'I'll never forget it,' I tell her. *'"Hope is the thing with feathers." But Clara—'*

'Was there anything strange about the page?'

'No, it was a beautiful page. But Clara—'

'Then perhaps I'm wrong,' says Clara, *'and it's not a code at all. If it was a code, one of the letters on page 7 would be marked, just as it was in Episode 6 of* Amelia X, Girl Detective.'

'You mean like the dot above the H?'

'There was a dot above the H? But you said there was nothing strange.'

'A dot is not strange, Clara. The world is full of dots, many of them edible.'

But she's no longer listening to me. She's poring over Delphine's letter and muttering to herself. *'H is the eighth letter in the alphabet. So perhaps if I read every eighth word ... And now it makes sense!'*

I'm confused. It seems there *is* a code. Could it be a *police* code?

'Clara—'

She pokes the letter with her claw. *'The writer wants Delphine to steal something valuable and sell it. But he doesn't say what the valuable thing is. If Constable Dad was here, I would show him our evidence. But he's away on a training course. So we will do more investigation while we wait for him to return.'*

'But Clara, Delphine is a police officer!'

Home-from-school o'clock

Clara has gone to find Olive, to tell her about Delphine. I have promised to tell Tracy about the secret code.

'Between us, we will solve this mystery,' said Clara.

Tracy doesn't yet know that we are going to solve a mystery. She is staring at a bit of paper.

I arrange my fridge letters on her pillow.

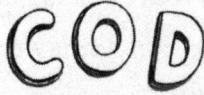

I nip Tracy's elbow, and point towards my message.

She wrinkles her face. 'You want fish for dinner? I think we're having sausages.'

I try again.

'You're cold?' says Tracy.

COAD

'You want a *coat*? You're a *duck*, Rita, you don't need a coat.'

Why are humans so bad at spelling? How can I tell her about the mystery if she doesn't understand my writing?

I am trying to puzzle it out when she mutters, 'I still haven't done this poem.'

I raise my head and stare at her.

She points at the bit of paper. 'It's homework. And it's due next week. We have to write an acrostic poem.'

I poke my head under her arm.

'See?' she says. 'We've got the first letter of each line, and we have to fill in the rest.'

I inspect the paper carefully.

Words come to me.

I glance around the room to make sure Great-Aunt Myrtle hasn't sneaked in.

Then I arrange my fridge letters on the paper.

FLY BESID ME
REST YOR WINGS
ON MINE
I WILL SUPORT
YOO
EVN THROO THE
STORM
NUTHING WILL
HARM YOO
BECOS I AM A
DUCK

My army reads it.

She reads it again.

A tear rolls down her face.

'That's beautiful, Rita,' she whispers. '"I will support you, even through the storm."'

She sniffs and wipes the tear away. She bites her lip. She sits up straight. 'I know I promised I wouldn't say anything. But Olive and I used to be really good friends. I have to tell her about Delphine.'

On-the-bike o'clock

I am in the basket and Tracy is pedalling hard. We whizz down the main street of Little Dismal—

And there are Olive and Digby, riding towards us. Clara is perched in the basket at the front of Olive's bike.

My basket is nicer than hers. But hers isn't bad.

We stop. So do they.

The humans look at the ground. Then they look at the sky. Then they look at the other side of the street, as if something interesting is happening over there.

'Why are they not talking to each other?' I ask Clara.

'Olive does not like Tracy,' she says. *'But they must talk to each other. It is important.'*

So I bite Tracy's hand.

She jumps. 'OW!'

Then she and Olive speak at the same time, 'It's about Delphine.'

Tracy's face goes red. She stares at the ground again. 'I was just coming to tell you,' she mumbles.

'Is she really a police officer?' asks Digby.

Tracy nods, but doesn't look up. 'Federal police. She's – she's investigating Olive's dad.'

Now it's Olive's turn to go red. 'Why would she be investigating Dad? He hasn't done anything wrong. And what about the letter?'

Tracy looks up at last. 'What letter?'

Digby takes it out of his pocket and hands it to her. 'The code that Clara worked out. You have to read every eighth word.'

'Didn't you tell her about the code?' asks Clara.

I don't want Clara to think that Tracy is bad at spelling. And besides, I *tried* to tell her.

'That's why we are here,' I say. *'Because of the code.'* Which is a*lmost* true.

Tracy is puzzling over the letter. 'Why would a federal police officer steal something?'

'Are you sure she's federal police?' asks Olive. 'Did she show you her badge?'

'No, she just told me,' says Tracy.

'And you believed her?'

Tracy bites her lip. 'I – yes. She said that Uncle Dylan was innocent.'

Digby snorts. 'Your uncle Dylan was selling drugs, Tracy. Everyone in Little Dismal knew about it.'

'I'm going to call Dad,' says Olive, taking a phone from her pocket.

'But—' says Tracy.

Olive glares at her. 'He hasn't done anything wrong.'

'Okay,' whispers Tracy.

Dad o'clock

Olive is talking to her phone. 'Yes,' she says. 'All right ... Yes, Dad ... I don't know ... It's in code, but Clara and Rita worked it out ... Tracy's duck ... Yeah, I think so.'

'Why is she telling her phone about me?' I ask Clara.

'She is not telling the phone. She is telling Constable Dad.'

Before I can ask my next question, she adds, *'He is not in the phone. He is in Melbourne. The phone is a long-distance squawk.'*

I knew that.

Olive puts her long-distance squawk in

her pocket and says, 'Dad's coming back tomorrow lunchtime. He'll sort it out then. And in the meantime he wants us to stay away from Delphine. I think he's worried that she might be dangerous.'

'She could not be as dangerous as a duck,' I murmur to Clara.

'Couldn't we at least follow her?' says Digby. 'If we were careful, she wouldn't see us. And we might find out what she's trying to steal.'

Olive shakes her head. 'He said we're not to go near her. He doesn't think she's federal police at all. He said that if he was being investigated, it'd be the Anti-Corruption Commission. But he's going to make some phone calls, just to check.'

Clara leans closer to my basket and murmurs, *'I will meet you at the compost heap tomorrow morning, Rita.'*

'You will? But—'

'This is our investigation,' she says. 'And we are not going to stop just because Constable Dad tells us to. We are going to find out what Delphine is up to.'

Friday
Little Dismal

To Jubilee Crystal Simpson
Somewhere on earth

Hi Jubilee, these have never been real letters, have they? I mean, I was never going to post them.

So I guess it doesn't matter if I write them in my head instead of on paper.

And it doesn't matter if I tell you things I'd never tell you in real life.

Like how scared I was this morning, when Delphine's car pulled up beside me on my way to school.

She wound down her window. 'Today's the day,

Marguerite,' she said. 'Constable Hennessey has covered his tracks too well. We're going to have to trap him into a confession.'

I didn't know what to do. We were supposed to stay away from her, but here she was!

'I know this isn't easy for you,' said Delphine. 'You're such a loyal, kind girl.'

She'd said stuff like that to me before. *Nice* stuff. And I'd thought she meant it.

But now I knew she didn't. It was what Mum calls 'buttering me up', so I'd do what she wanted me to do.

I almost said, 'No, I'm not. I'm horrible. I'm trying to be kind, but it doesn't always work.'

But Delphine was still talking. 'The thing is, Marguerite, sometimes I hate what I have to do. But it's my duty. I put the bad people in prison. I make sure that the good ones – like your uncle Dylan – get justice.'

'Mum thinks Uncle Dylan's a nasty piece of work,' I mumbled.

'Well, of course she does,' said Delphine. 'Constable Hennessey made it look that way.' She reached out the window and put her hand on my arm. 'And you're the only one who can help me fix it.'

'I don't know—'

Delphine let go of my arm and sat back in her seat. She swallowed, as if she was trying not to cry.

'I thought we were friends,' she said. 'I thought I had found someone I could rely on. Someone who would help me, even when things got hard. I know you're just a kid, Marguerite, but I recognised something in you as soon as we met. Something that reminded me of myself when I was your age. Quick-witted, clever, always a step ahead of everyone else. Was I wrong? Are you going to let me down when I'm so close to success?'

Yes, *definitely* buttering me up. But that 'so close to success' worried me. Olive's dad wasn't due back until lunchtime. What if Delphine got away before he could arrest her?

And what was she going to *do?* Why was she talking about a trap, when she was supposed to be here to steal something?

'Constable Hennessey's in Melbourne,' I said.

Delphine sat up straight. 'Even better. We'll have time to set the trap properly before he returns.' She smiled at me. 'I don't want to involve you more than I have to. But here's the deal. Hennessey's daughter really loves that chook of hers, doesn't she?'

'Clara?'

'Don't worry, I won't hurt her. I'm just going to use her as a bargaining tool. As soon as Hennessey confesses his crimes, I'll let her go.'

The valuable thing in the letter – it was *Clara!* Delphine was going to steal her and sell her!

'So, will you come with me?' she asked. 'Will you help me?'

'Now?' I said.

'Yes, right now.'

I knew it was dangerous, going with her. And I'm not a brave person. I never have been. But I wanted to show Olive that I'd changed. I wanted to make up for all the horrible things I'd done to her.

I wanted to save Clara.

'Okay,' I said.

Delphine smiled. 'Excellent. Put your bike in the boot and hop in.'

From Tracy

Frightday

Meeting-up-with-Clara o'clock

I am a poet. I am also a detective. As soon as I land at Clara's secret headquarters, we start doing important detective stuff.

'I have been thinking about who wrote the letter,' she says. *'A code like this is the work of a master criminal. And what well-known master criminal has the same initials as Eddie Smythe? Ernie Simpson!'*

That name is familiar. *'The human who stole the sheep? The one you arrested?'*

'Yes,' says Clara. *'He is in prison, so if he wants to send secret instructions to his gang,*

he must write in code. Otherwise the prison officers will read it and stop his evil plans.'

'You think Delphine is his gang?'

'I do.' Clara scratches the side of her head with a claw. *'In episode 22 of* Death in the City, *Inspector Garcia had Unfinished Business. Now I also have Unfinished Business. What is the valuable object Delphine is going to sell? Did Ernie Simpson bury his ill-gotten gains somewhere in Little Dismal? Is there a stash of stolen jewels in the basement of the Dismal Arms Hotel? Or a suitcase full of banknotes?'*

'Or a book of poems written by a duck,' I say. 'We should search her room again.'

'It's not the book,' says Clara. *'But we should certainly search the hotel. Come along.'*

We fly to the hotel in short bursts, which is all Clara can manage.

I am not at all impatient.

I am not *very* impatient.

I am not—

I fly beside her. I try to support her wings with mine.

It doesn't work nearly as well in real life as it did in my poem.

Quarter past oops

At last we land in the yard behind the hotel. Clara is covered in dust, and several of her feathers are broken. When I try to help her again, she snaps at me.

'*All right, all right,*' I say, backing away. '*You search Delphine's room on your own.*'

'*I'm not going to search her room,*' says Clara. '*I'm going to search the basement.*' And she stalks away.

I decide that *I* will search Delphine's room instead. And if I happen to find a book of poems written by a duck, I will take it as evidence.

Friday
Little Dismal

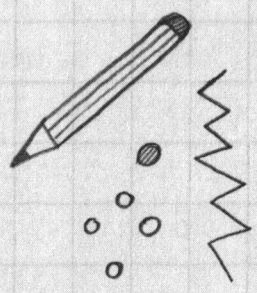

To Jubilee Crystal Simpson
Somewhere on earth

Hi Jubilee, I was pretty scared, but I didn't want Delphine to see it.

So I did my best to look keen.

She drove us to Olive's place. 'This is where the chook usually hangs out at this time of morning?'

'I think so,' I said.

'Good, this is what we're going to do. You'll go into the yard and call the chook, and when you've caught her, I'll bring the cage.'

I couldn't help myself. I squeaked, 'Cage?'

'It's just temporary,' said Delphine. 'Just until Constable Hennessey confesses to the crimes that have hurt so many innocent people.' She glanced at me and smiled. 'Don't worry, I'll look after her very well.'

I jumped out of the car. 'Okay.'

At first, I hoped that Clara wasn't there. Then I hoped she was there, so I could warn her.

But there was no sign of her in the backyard. I stood beside the compost heap, trying to work out what I should do now. How could I warn Clara? How could I tell Olive and Digby what was happening? If only I had my phone—

The Hennesseys' phone!

No one in Little Dismal locks their back door. I ran straight through the kitchen and into the hallway, where Olive and I used to play Barbies. And there was the landline.

I couldn't remember Olive's number, so I phoned Mum.

I got her voicemail.

'Answer your phone, Mum,' I whispered. 'Answer your phone!'

But she didn't.

Constable Hennessey's number was on the wall. I tried that too, my fingers trembling on the buttons.

More voicemail.

'Constable Hennessey,' I said, 'it's Tracy here, you've got to come back straight away, Delphine's trying to steal Clara—'

A hand snatched the phone away from me and slammed it down.

'You little idiot,' snarled Delphine. 'I knew I couldn't trust you.' She grabbed my arm and shook me. 'Who else did you call?'

'N-no one.'

'Who. Else. Did. You. Call?'

'I – I called Mum. B-but she wasn't answering.'

Delphine's eyes flickered from one side of the hall to the other, as if she was thinking hard. 'Right,' she said. And she dragged me outside.

She must've been in the Hennesseys' yard before, because she dragged me straight to the toolshed.

Pushed me through the door and shot the bolt, so I was locked in.

Her footsteps crunched over the gravel path. A moment later, I heard her car drive away.

From Tracy

Frightday

Breaking-and-entering o'clock

Delphine's room looks different.

Why is it different?

And where is the book?

It's not in the wardrobe, where it was before. It's not under the nest. It's not on the nest.

'This is important evidence,' I say to the room. *'What have you done with it?'*

The room does not answer. But as I head for the wardrobe once again, my eye falls on Delphine's suitcase, filled to the brim with human things.

I empty it. And there's the book, right at the bottom.

It is not easy flying out the window with a book in my beak, but I manage it on my third try.

I would like to stop and read the feather poem again. But I'm a detective now, as well as a poet, and I must tell Clara about the changes in the room. So I drop the book behind the water tank where no one will see it and steal it. Then I hop down the basement stairs.

The room at the bottom is full of boxes. Clara is investigating each one, pecking little holes in them to see what's inside.

'No jewels yet,' she says. 'No banknotes, either. And there are no signs of digging, so I do not think Ernie Simpson buried any bodies here. Did you find anything interesting in the suspect's room?'

'The wardrobe is empty. And the book of poems was in a suitcase filled with clothes and things.'

Clara stares at me. 'The suspect has packed her clothes? She's leaving? I must go and see. You stay in the yard and keep watch.'

She races for the stairs and flutters up them, three at a time. I follow her. I will keep watch behind the water tank, with my book of poems.

Half past Emily-Duckinson

I am dizzy with poems. There are so many of them. I can't read most of them yet, but that doesn't matter. If it wasn't for Clara, I wouldn't have found them.

Perhaps, between us, we can make it look as if I took revenge on her.

Then Great-Aunt Myrtle will be happy.

And so will I.

Finding this book has
Rearranged my life.
I will not hide my talent
Every duck will hear of me—

I am interrupted by a flurry of wings as someone lands behind me.

It's Vera.

I push the book underneath the tank stand and try to look as if I was not thinking about poetry.

'Um – hi, Vera,' I say.

She doesn't even bother saying hello. *'Great-Aunt Myrtle wants to know what's going on.*

We haven't heard from you in days. And the cows are still laughing at us.'

She leans towards me with a threatening expression. *'Where's the revenge, Rita? What have you been doing all this time?'*

I'd like to tell her that I have changed my mind about taking revenge on Clara.

I'd like to tell her that I am a poet. And a detective.

But when I think of Great-Aunt Myrtle, the words will not come out of my beak.

Instead, I find myself saying, *'I have been setting a trap.'*

Vera eyes me suspiciously. *'What sort of trap?'*

'A very complicated trap. And if you are here, it will not work. So please go away before you spoil everything.'

She doesn't move.

A car drives into the hotel yard.

A *blue* car.

Friday
Little Dismal

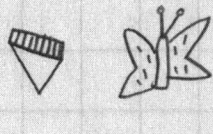

To Jubilee Crystal Simpson
Somewhere on earth

Dear Jubilee, Olive and I used to hide in the toolshed when we were little.

We used to squeeze through a gap in the back wall, under the workbench.

The gap was still there, but I'm a lot bigger than I was back then. So I set to work making the gap bigger too.

I wrenched at the wood. I found Constable Hennessey's hammer and bashed at the old, rusty nails. I accidentally hammered my thumb, and it hurt like crazy. But I didn't stop.

Because Delphine hadn't looked like someone who was about to give up and go away.

She'd looked angry. And desperate.

And I was the only one who knew what she was trying to do.

As soon as the hole was big enough, I crawled through it. I ripped the sleeve of my school shirt on one of the nails, and there were scratches all over my legs. But none of that mattered.

My bike was still in the boot of Delphine's car.

So I started running.

From Tracy

Frightday

Blue car o'clock

Delphine climbs out of her car and walks into the hotel.

This is where I am supposed to quack a warning.

But Vera is still suspicious. If I start shouting things like, *'Enemy approaching!'* and *'Action stations!'* she'll know that I'm warning someone. She'll investigate, and discover that I'm working with our sworn enemy.

She'll tell Great-Aunt Myrtle.

My legs go weak at the thought.

All the same, I can't just stand here and do

nothing. So I say, as loudly as I dare, *'Look at that BLUE CAR! What an interesting-looking BLUE CAR! I wonder who drives that BLUE CAR?'*

Vera takes a step back. *'Why are you talking like that? Have you caught a disease? Have you eaten something bad?'*

I'm just about to say, *'Yes, so you had better leave—'* when the window of Delphine's room slams shut.

I hear a muffled squawk.

Vera's head snaps around. *'That was a chook.'*

Another squawk from Clara, much louder this time.

Vera and I peep around the edge of the water tank, just in time to see Delphine hurrying out the back door of the hotel.

She's carrying something wrapped up in a cloth.

Something alive.

Something that kicks and struggles and squawks.

She's-stealing-Clara o'clock!

'Help! Help!' squawks Clara.

'Shut up, chook,' mutters Delphine.

She opens the back door of the blue car. There's a cage on the back seat, and Delphine thrusts the bundle into it, pulls the cloth away and shuts the cage door.

I catch a glimpse of Clara, still crying for help. Then Delphine throws the cloth over the cage.

Clara falls silent.

'Well, well, well,' says Vera. *'So you were telling the truth about a trap. Congratulations, Rita, very clever. I didn't think you had it in you.'*

'But that's not—' I begin. Then I stop. How can I tell her that I want to rescue Clara, not get rid of her?

'Good to see that you've forgotten about that poetry nonsense and returned to proper duck business,' says Vera. *'I'll go and tell Great-Aunt Myrtle, shall I? Reckon she'll be pleased.'*

She doesn't wait for an answer, but takes a short run-up and flies away.

I turn back to the car.

The door is shut. Delphine is hurrying into the hotel.

What-do-I-do-now o'clock?

Perhaps I should attack the car. If it was a cow I wouldn't hesitate. But cars are made of harder stuff than cows.

So instead, I run out from behind the water tanks and throw myself into the air.

Tracy. I must find Tracy.

Friday
Little Dismal

To Jubilee Crystal Simpson
Somewhere on earth

Dear Jubilee, by the time I got to the hotel, I had the most awful stitch in my side.

There were a few people around now, but I didn't stop. It'd take too long to explain, and I didn't have time.

I had to get to school. I had to find Clara and make sure she was safe. I had to find Olive.

But just as I ran past the hotel verandah, Rita came flying around the corner. When she saw me, she did a kind of midair somersault and crash-landed in front of me.

'Rita,' I gasped. 'Have you seen Clara?'

She tore open the bag around her neck and scattered the fridge letters on the ground.

DELFIN STEEL CLARA CAGE CAR

'She's caught her?' I squeaked.

DELFIN LEVING TAK CLARA

'She's leaving already?'

My head was spinning. I had to get to school. I had to tell Olive. But if Delphine was leaving...

'Rita, go to school and tell Olive. As fast as you

can. Tell her – I don't know – just tell her to come! I'm going to try and free Clara.'

Rita took off, and the fridge letters flew in all directions. I left them where they were and raced around the back of the hotel.

From Tracy

Frightday

School o'clock

The front door of the school is closed. But as I fly around one side, a child opens a classroom window.

I swoop past him and he screams with fright. The teacher cries, 'Where did that duck come from?'

But I am already out the door and into the corridor.

Teachers and students dive to one side as I flap past them. One of the teachers tries to catch me, so I do a quick pivot and kick in midair, and leave her gasping on the floor.

And there at last is Olive's room. I fly straight through the door and land on her desk.

She gasps. The whole class gasps.

I pick up a pen from Olive's desk.

It breaks.

'Rita,' says Olive. 'What are you doing here?'

She tries to grab me. Out of respect for Clara, I don't attack her.

Instead, I fly out of reach, to the front of the classroom. And there, right where I need it, is a white board to write on. And a large black pen!

I will not break this pen. I will not break this pen. I will *NOT*—

Oops.

But there's a green pen as well.

I pick it up as gently as I can. I bite the top off.

Mrs Savage is advancing on me with a determined expression. Her arms are outstretched. She does not look as if she will be easily beaten, not even with a block, pivot and kick.

I teeter on the ledge in front of the white board.

I write.

CLARA

Mrs Savage stops. She turns to look at Olive – who is standing up from her desk with a worried expression.

'What about Clara?' says Olive. 'Has something happened to her?'

'Will you be my boyfriend?'

Olive's face turns as white as a feather. 'Where is she?'

Now this is something I know how to write.

STOLN BY DELFIN

'Stolen?' squeaks Olive. 'By – is that Delphine?'

'Will you be my boyfriend?'

Mrs Savage looks at me, then at Olive. 'There must be some misunderstanding. Delphine's a journalist. I don't believe for a moment that she would—'

But Olive is already racing out the door.

'Olive!' shouts Mrs Savage. 'Come back here!'

Olive doesn't stop.

'Digby, go after her,' says Mrs Savage. 'Whatever she thinks she's going to do, stop her. I'll phone her father.'

'He's in Melbourne at a training course,' says Digby. 'Olive's staying with me.'

Mrs Savage shakes her head. 'I'll phone him anyway. Now go after Olive and make sure she doesn't do anything silly.'

Digby jumps to his feet and runs out of the classroom. I want to go too, but there's one more thing I must write.

TRACY GON TO FREE CLARA

'Oh my goodness,' cries Mrs Savage. 'I'd better call Tracy's mother too!'

Friday
Little Dismal

To Jubilee Crystal Simpson
Somewhere on earth

Hi Jubilee, the doors of Delphine's car were locked, so I peered through the window.

There was something on the back seat. Something big enough to be a cage, but it was covered with a blanket, so I couldn't be sure.

Except for the single white chook feather on the floor of the car.

I knew I should run and get someone. But what if Delphine drove away while I was gone? What if Clara was lost forever because of me?

I heard footsteps and dived behind the water tank. Out of the hotel came Delphine, carrying a suitcase.

She opened the boot of the car, dragged my bike out and dumped it on the ground. Then she chucked the suitcase in, shut the boot, wheeled my bike around the corner out of sight, and hurried back inside the hotel.

My mouth felt as if I'd been eating gravel. Because Delphine *thought* she'd shut the boot. But she hadn't. Not quite.

I stared at it. I still didn't feel brave.

But I had to do *something*.

When Mr Simpson tried to escape with the stolen sheep, Clara hid in the back of the truck.

'Be like Clara,' I whispered to myself.

I took off my sandals and left them by the tank, so Rita would know I'd been there.

I raced across the yard. I pulled the boot open, climbed in, and pulled it shut again. Properly shut.

Just in time. Someone hurried out of the hotel.

The footsteps sounded like Delphine's.

She opened the car door, and the car jolted a little as she climbed in.

The door shut. The car started.

We drove away.

Tracy

Frightday

Why-are-humans-so-slow o'clock?

Arms are not nearly as good as wings. Why do humans insist on having them? If Olive and Digby could fly, they would be at the hotel in no time.

As it is, I get there well ahead of them and land beside the back door.

The first thing I notice is that Delphine's car is gone.

So is Clara.

And there's no sign of Tracy.

I race around the yard three times, just in case they are hiding under a bush. *'Tracy!'*

I quack. *'Clara, where have you gone?'*

They do not answer.

My feathers are ruffled. My heart is beating too fast.

I compose a quick poem to calm myself down.

***F**ind Tracy and Clara!*
***R**ight. But how?*
***I** don't know.*
***E**ven poetry can't help me*
***N**ow.*
***D**rat!*

What would General Ya do, if two of her friends went missing in suspicious circumstances?

First she would check for dead bodies, in case her friends had come to a bad end. Then she would tear the town apart until she found them.

I start with Delphine's room.

There are no dead bodies, so I concentrate on tearing the nest apart. The destruction makes me feel a lot better, and by the time Olive and Digby run into the yard, panting, I have worked out my next move.

I must search the town.

But before I can begin, a car drives into the yard. Is it Delphine?

No, it's Mum, who is a spy. That could come in handy.

Sitting next to her is Sweetheart. And to my relief, Second and Third Army are in the back seat.

Mum leaps out of the car, crying, 'Where is she? What's happened to my daughter?'

Shouldn't a spy already know this sort of thing? Perhaps she is not a very good spy.

Sweetheart climbs out too, and spots me on the windowsill. 'Is that Rita? What's she doing here?'

'She's the one who told us about Delphine stealing Clara,' says Digby. 'She said Tracy had gone after them.'

Mum puts her hand over her mouth and makes a squeaking sound. Sweetheart grabs her other hand and says, 'Don't worry, we'll find her.'

Then he turns to Digby. 'What do you mean, *Rita* told you?'

'The duck?' whispers Mum.

They are staring at me now. So I nod my head. *'Will you be my boyfriend?'*

Mum gasps. 'She understands! She's like Clara!'

Of course I am not like Clara. She is a chook. I am a duck. She is a detective, I am a poet.

These are major differences.

But I forgive Mum, because she is worried about Tracy.

So am I.

By now, Second and Third Army have

escaped from the car and are roaming around the yard.

No one else has noticed. I decide to take advantage of this fact.

While Mum, Sweetheart, Olive and Digby try to work out where Tracy has gone, I follow Second and Third Army behind the water tank.

'Now listen, troops,' I begin.

But then I stop. Because there, right in front of me, are Tracy's sandals.

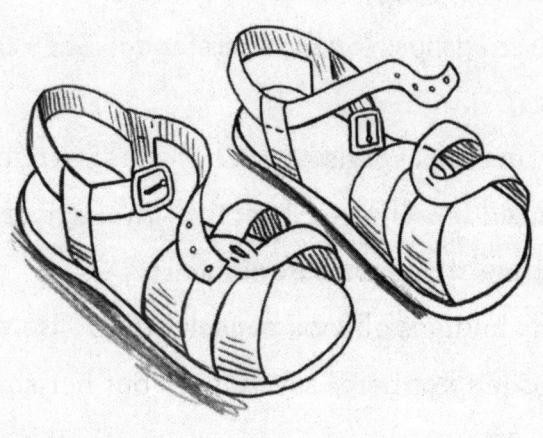

Tracy is not wearing them.

For a moment, I forget where I am. I imagine I am back on the pond, in the early days of my training, when we first learned about the General Alert.

'Enemy activity spotted!' I quack. *'Action stations! Prepare for battle!'*

But instead of an army of ducks, I find myself surrounded by humans.

Mum sees the sandals and makes that squeaking noise again. 'They're Tracy's! But – but what are they doing here?'

'Maybe she left them for us to find,' says Olive. 'So we'd know…'

'Know what?' asks Digby.

'Could she have gone in the car with Delphine?' demands Sweetheart.

The humans all look at each other.

'If she's not here,' says Olive, 'but her shoes are…'

I don't wait to hear anymore. I take to the air.

Half past where's-Tracy?

I fly up.

   I fly up and up and up.

And up and up and up and up and up. Higher than I have ever been in my life.

Then I find a spiral of warm air and float on it, peering in every direction.

Delphine can't have been gone for long. Somewhere, on one of the roads out of Little Dismal, there must be a car.

A blue car...

A blue car! There it is, heading south!

I drop out of the sky so fast that I nearly go into a spin. But I manage to pull myself up at the last moment, and lose nothing but a few feathers.

'They're heading south!' I quack. *'Follow me!'*

They stare up at me. *'What's she saying?'* asks Mum.

'South!' I shout. *'S-O-W-T-H – oh for goodness sake!'*

I fly a quick loop above them, then make myself into an arrow pointing south. *'Get it?'* I shout as I whizz overhead.

No, they don't get it.

I do it again.

Olive gets it! (Clara has trained her well.) 'I think Rita's seen Delphine's car,' she cries. 'She's going to lead the way!'

They pile into Mum's car. I take careful note of what it looks like from above, so as not to lose it.

Then I set off to follow Tracy.

Friday
somewhere on the highway heading south

Dear Jubilee, I'm scared. I'm all squashed up against Delphine's suitcase, with the handle poking into my arm, and there's something jabbing at my leg. I think it's the jack, though it's dark, so I can't see it.

I don't usually mind the dark.

I can cry in the dark.

I can be angry, without anyone else knowing.

Sometimes I feel as if I'm full of darkness, and there's no way any light can get in – at least, I used to feel like that.

Before Rita came.

Isn't it funny how one little duck can change

things? Or maybe she didn't really change them, she just made me look at them differently.

Like, I thought it was dancing, but it turned out to be unarmed combat.

I thought Mum hated me. But she didn't.

I thought Delphine was my friend. But she wasn't.

Being in the boot gives me a lot of time to think. Some of the things I think of make me cringe. Make me realise I owe Olive Hennessey more than one apology.

Maybe a dozen.

Or a hundred.

That's why I'm here. To make it up to her.

And when I'm not thinking about Mum or Rita or Olive, I'm trying to work out what I'm going to do when Delphine opens the boot and finds me curled around her suitcase.

Smile?

Burst into tears?

Jump up and shout, 'Surprise!'?

I wish I could go back a couple of weeks and make this never happen.

From Tracy

Frightday

Heading-south o'clock

Aunt Charlene is the only duck on the pond who has ever been to the city. She still has nightmares about it.

She says the city was huge and terrible. She says there were far too many humans and cars, and they all looked alike.

She says she flew for hours and nearly fainted with exhaustion before she found her way to the edge of it.

But Aunt Charlene is known to exaggerate, so I'm not worried. I expect the city will be bigger than Little Dismal. Perhaps three streets, instead of one. Or even four!

Which means I will have to keep a close eye on Delphine's car, in case it is not the only blue one on those streets.

We-have-come-to-the-city o'clock!
It *is* bigger than Little Dismal, just as I suspected. There are *five* streets – no wonder Aunt Charlene was confused.

Delphine's car slows down, and I circle over it, wondering where she will stop, and how I will free Tracy and Clara.

Best keep it simple. I will attack Delphine as soon as she opens the door.

But the blue car does not stop. It drives right through the city and out the other side – and now it is speeding up again.

I check that Mum's car is still following me. I dip my wings to let them know I have seen them. I fly on.

Half past there-is-more-than-one-city
Aunt Charlene never told us that there was more than one city. So far I have counted four.

There is bigger than I ever knew.

Getting-tired o'clock
My wings are growing tired and I am hungry, but I cannot stop to rest or catch a quick snack. Delphine's car is still beetling along the road below, and my friends are trapped inside it.

I hope we come to the right city soon.

Half past tired-and-hungry
I can see some more houses ahead. They are bigger than the houses in Little Dismal. Perhaps some of them will be even bigger than the Dismal Arms Hotel—

Oh.

I have reached the city.

There are more than five streets.

There is more than one blue car ... and suddenly I'm not sure which one I'm supposed to be following!

Is it *that* one?

Or *that* one?

Or – or *that* one?

The noise and the stink of the city swamp my senses.

I *think* it's that one...

Aunt-Charlene-was-right o'clock

The blue car stops, and a human gets out. I am bracing myself to swoop down and attack her – when I realise it is not Delphine.

I have followed the wrong car!

I fly in desperate circles, but although I find any number of blue cars, Delphine is not in any of them.

I have failed. My only hope now is to

tell Mum what has happened. Perhaps she knows things about the city that I do not. Perhaps she can find Tracy and Clara, where I cannot.

Oh.

I cannot find Mum's car either.

But I will not panic.
I will *not* panic.
I will not panic I will not panic I will not will not not not not…

Panic o'clock

Help! Aunt Charlene! Great-Aunt Myrtle! Vera! Anyone!

Heeeeeeeeeeeeeeeelp!

Friday
Melbourne, I think
(because there are trams)

Hey Jubilee, do you live in a city?

I don't know how you could bear it. It's so noisy. Trams dinging and rumbling. People shouting. Cars everywhere, some of them so close that I'm scared they'll run right into me. And then I'll never get the chance to shout, 'Surprise!'

Ha ha. Joke.

There are smells, too. Car smells, making me choke. Food smells, whizzing past my nose before I can grab them.

I'm so hungry. And thirsty. And scared—

Hang on, I think we're going down a ramp. It feels different from the street. Quieter. Darker.

And now we've stopped. Not just at a traffic light. Stopped completely. Engine off.

My foot's cramping. My tummy's so empty I'd eat anything, even tinned spaghetti, which I hate.

Delphine's car door opens and she gets out. I brace myself.

But she doesn't open the boot, she just stands there. She must be using her phone, because I hear her say, 'I'm in the underground car park, Ashlee. Come down and help.'

Then she leans against the car (I feel it move) and waits.

I wait, too.

A lift rumbles. A door opens and shuts. Footsteps walk towards us.

A voice says, 'Why can't you do it yourself? Why do I always have to carry stuff?'

I know that voice.

I know it really well. Though it no longer has an American accent.

It's you, Jubilee.
It's you.

from Tracy

Frightday

Half past panic

I flap back and forth, quacking as loudly as I can.

No one comes to help me. I am lost in the city. There is only one thing to do.

I make up a poem.

<u>A poem of despair</u>
The city is big
and I am small.
Alas, poor Rita.
Who will mourn me
if I die here

friendless
and alone?

This does not make me feel better. But at least I have achieved someth—

I hear wings in the distance, and look around.

Ducks! A whole flock of them, flying deeper into the city!

My heart jolts. *'Wait for me!'* I quack.

They ignore me.

So I fly after them.

Friday
MELBOURNE

Dear Mum, I can't write to Jubilee anymore. Not even in my head. Not when she's right here in front of me.

So I'm going to imagine I'm writing to you instead. Otherwise I might just start crying.

I wish you were here, Mum. You and Laurie and the twins. And Rita. I'd give anything to see you all walk through that hotel door.

But it's not going to happen.

It's just me and Jubilee Crystal Simpson.

Except that's not her name.

She's Ashlee. She was Ashlee all along.

And Delphine is her mother.

I tried to pretend that I still believed in them, Mum. I couldn't think of what else to do.

And besides, I was scared.

So even before the boot opened, I started to cry.

At least, I *pretended* to cry. Loudly.

Jubilee squeaked, 'What's that?' (I'm going to keep calling her Jubilee, because that's how I think of her.)

Delphine shushed her, and whispered something.

Then the boot flew open, and there was my best friend.

Ha ha.

'Jubilee!' I said. I rubbed my eyes so they couldn't tell I hadn't really been crying. 'What are you doing here? How do you know Delphine? Are you helping her bring Constable Hennessey to justice?'

I didn't give either of them time to answer. I figured I had to tell them exactly what I was thinking, so they'd know how to act.

'I'm sorry, Delphine,' I babbled. 'I'm sorry I didn't help you catch Olive's chook. I realised almost straight away that I *should* have helped, because you're helping Uncle Dylan. And I want to be part of it, I really do! So I sort of stowed away. I hope you don't mind. I mean, I could be really helpful!'

It didn't work.

Delphine glared at me. Then she glared at Jubilee. 'I thought you said this kid was stupid. I thought you said she'd be easy to fool.'

'She is,' said Jubilee. 'You must've done something wrong. It's not my fault.'

I swallowed the lump in my throat. I guess Jubilee was never my friend. Not really.

'Well, she's here now,' snapped Delphine. 'So what are you going to do about it?'

'Me?' said Jubilee.

'Yes, you. I can't put her out on the street, she's already tried to phone the police once.

Just keep her out of my way for a few hours. And make sure she doesn't talk to anyone.'

All this time, I was lying in the boot, so stiff and cramped and sore that I couldn't move.

Delphine loomed over me. 'I don't know what you think you're doing here. But if you cause me the least bit of trouble, the chook will suffer. Do you understand me? I said, *do you understand me?*'

My mouth dried up. She was so angry.

I nodded.

They had to help me out of the boot, and I started crying again, only this time it was real.

Jubilee rolled her eyes. 'Loser.'

'Take her up to your room,' said Delphine. 'I'll bring the chook up shortly. I want to be out of here by nightfall.'

So that's where I am, Mum. In Jubilee's room, which has a connecting door to Delphine's.

I wish I could think of something brilliant to do. Or even a tiny bit clever. But I can't.

Delphine's going to sell Clara, and I don't know how to save her.

Love from Tracy

Frightday

The-city-is-even-bigger-than-I-realised o'clock

The houses go on and on, until we reach a place where they stick up into the sky like fence posts.

(Only a lot bigger.)

And then it keeps going on.

But the city ducks seem to know where they're heading. They swoop between the giant fence posts and begin to lose height.

And there, just ahead of us, is a small patch of countryside.

There are trees! And bushes! And grass!

Best of all, there is a pond.

The city ducks circle the pond, then come in to land with their wings turning in backward circles and their feet outstretched.

They are still ignoring me. But they are my only chance of finding Tracy and Clara, so I circle the pond, too.

It is not my best landing. My backward circles are as smooth as I can make them. My feet are stretched out at just the right angle. The water parts beneath me, and I begin to slow down.

But I am distracted. There are ducks all around me. Strange ducks. And every single one of them is staring at me.

They do not look friendly.

Consequently, I do not notice how quickly I am approaching the far side of the pond...

Just past overshoot

By the time I have tumbled to a halt, turned

myself up the right way and shaken the mud and leaves out of my feathers, there is a duck standing right in front of me.

She glares down her beak. *'Who are you? And what are you doing on our pond?'*

She sounds just like Great-Aunt Myrtle. Fierce and bossy.

I crouch low. *'My name's Rita, ma'am. I've just flown in from Little Dismal.'*

'Never heard of it,' she snaps.

'It's north-west of here,' I explain. *'Half a day's flying, and that's with a tail wind.'*

The great-aunt says nothing, so I quickly add, *'The ducks of Little Dismal send their best wishes, ma'am. And they were wondering – I mean, I was wondering – we were all wondering if you had seen Delphine's blue car.'*

She looks at me for a very long time. Then she says, *'What's it worth?'*

'Pardon?'

'What's it worth? What do we get out of it,

if we tell you where Delphine's blue car is?'

'Um – our thanks?'

The whole flock bursts out laughing.

'She's got to be kidding.'

'She thinks she can pay us in gratitude?'

'Next she'll be offering friendship!'

I can't afford to be offended. I can't afford to storm away.

So I keep my head low, and when the laughter stops, I say, *'What can I offer?'*

'Fish eggs,' says the great-aunt. *'And salamanders.'*

'Berries,' says another duck. *'A good beakfull of them.'*

'I rather fancy some of those nice goldfish from the western park,' says another.

And suddenly they are all talking, one on top of the other, demanding tadpoles and weeds and worms and grain and algae-but-not-that-nasty-stuff-from-the-fountain-I-mean-the-*nice*-algae.

I gulp. *'If I can get you these things, will you tell me where Delphine's car is?'*

'If you can get us these things, we'll tell you everything we know about Delphine's car,' says the great-aunt.

Keeping-my-side-of-the-bargain o'clock

I fly back and forth across the city, following the directions the ducks have given me. I find the tadpoles and the weeds, and race back with them, only to be told they are the wrong sort.

I find the salamanders, but they are apparently too small. (The great-aunt eats them all the same.)

I find the wrong grain, the wrong fish eggs, the wrong berries and the wrong algae (even though it's not the nasty stuff from the fountain).

So I check the directions and try again.

This time, the salamanders are big enough, but I have only brought two, instead of three.

(I thought the great-aunt asked for two. But I am so tired and hungry that I am probably mistaken.)

I go back for another salamander.

I accidentally eat it myself.

I go back for *another* salamander. When I deliver it to the great-aunt, she wants to know where the fish eggs are.

I go looking for the fish eggs. And the goldfish. And the worms and grain and – and I have forgotten what else.

But at last I have given the city ducks everything they asked for. Even the right algae.

I lie beside the pond for a moment or two, panting. My wings feel as if they are about to fall off. All I want to do is crawl under a bush and sleep for days.

But as soon as I have caught my breath, I stumble back to the water and paddle across to where the great-aunt is chatting with her friends.

'Excuse me, ma'am,' I croak.

She stares at me. *'Are you still here?'*

'Yes, ma'am. You promised you'd tell me everything you know about Delphine's car,' I say.

'And so I shall.' She raises her voice. *'Gather around, everyone. I'm going to tell our little cousin here everything we know about Delphine's car.'*

The other ducks paddle towards us from the corners of the pond.

They surround us.

They fall still.

I can hardly breathe. All of this work will be worth it, just as soon as I get the information I need.

The great-aunt flaps her wings in a commanding fashion. She dips her head into the water and takes a drink. Then she fixes me with one eye and says, *'What do we know about Delphine's car? Zilch.'*

This is a word I have never heard before. *'I beg your pardon, ma'am?'*

'Nada,' she says.

Another strange word. *'I don't understand, ma'am. Zilch and nada – are they places in the city?'*

One of the ducks behind me sniggers. The great-aunt nods thoughtfully and says, *'Perhaps.'*

More sniggers. If I wasn't so tired I might be able to work out why they are laughing. But I can't.

So I say, *'Please, ma'am, tell me what these words mean. Tell me what you know about Delphine's car.'*

The great-aunt peers around at her flock. *'Poor little duck doesn't understand. Shall we tell her what these words mean? Shall we tell her what we know about Delphine's car?'*

'Yes, yes, yes!' quack the other ducks.

'All together now,' says the great-aunt. 'One, two, three—'

'NOTHING,' shout the ducks. 'Zilch, nada, NOTHING! Ha ha ha ha ha ha ha ha ha ha ha ha ha ha ha ha ha ha ha ha ha ha ha ha ha ha ha ha ha ha ha ha ha ha ha ha ha ha ha ha ha ha ha ha ha ha ha ha ha ha ha ha ha ha ha ha ha ha ha ha ha ha ha ha ha ha ha ha ha ha ha ha ha ha ha ha ha ha ha ha ha ha ha ha ha ha ha ha!'

Friday
Melbourne

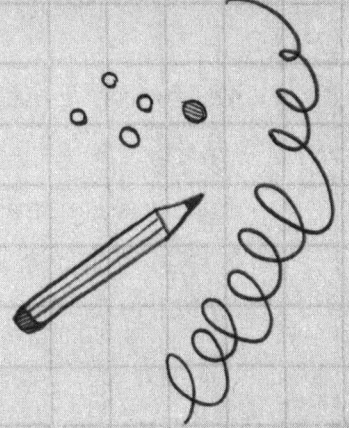

Dear Mum, I wish Jubilee would put her phone down, and go out for a couple of minutes. But it's always either in her hand or in her pocket. And she never leaves me alone.

When I sneak a look at her, she looks bored and angry.

Clara is still in the cage, and the cage is in the bathroom. Delphine gave her something to eat and drink, then put the blanket back.

I can't stop thinking about her. (Clara, not Delphine.) I hope she's not too scared. I hope she realises I'm trying to help.

I don't know what Delphine's doing. She was

in the next room, but then I think she went out.

I wish I knew what to do.

I wish I was smarter.

I wish I was braver.

I wish you and Laurie were here.

Love from Tracy

Frightday

I-thought-I-knew-despair o'clock

I cannot move. I cannot swim or fly or even raise my wings to block out the sound of their laughter.

All that work for nothing. All that hope, all those tadpoles, and I am no closer to finding Tracy and Clara than I was before.

I thought I knew despair.

But I did not.

As the laughter dies away, I throw caution to the wind and cry,

'A poem of despair: second verse

The city is cold
and the chill has reached my heart.
Alas, poor Rita.
Who will remember me
when I am dead
and gone?'

Before I have finished the third line, the laughter stops. Every eye is focused on me.

I don't care. After all, what more can they do? Laugh at me again? Tell me that ducks don't write poetry? Tell me I am a disgrace?

I already know those things.

I summon the last of my strength and paddle away from them.

To my dismay, they follow me. They jostle around me.

I swim faster. Perhaps, if I try very hard, I will even be able to lift off from the pond and fly.

But where will I go? The city is so big and loud and…

I raise my wings – and lower them again. The great-aunt has paddled right in front of me, so close that there's no room to take off.

She glares at me accusingly. *'You are a poet.'*

I will not deny it. *'Yes.'*

All around me, ducks are flapping their wings and muttering under their breath. They crowd against me. They stare at me.

Then the great-aunt says, *'Why didn't you tell us?'*

And suddenly I'm surrounded by voices.

'Our poet died ages ago.'

'We haven't heard a decent poem since then.'

'Tell us another one. Pleeeease tell us another poem!'

Half past why-didn't-you-tell-us?

Apparently there is more than one list.

The city ducks have 'poetry' on theirs.

It comes right after 'chasing dogs and cats'.

'The ducks on the southern dams have a completely different list to us,' says the great-aunt. She looks around at her companions. *'And that country duck from the far west – remember the one who got blown off course a while back, and ended up here? Her list was different again, wasn't it? Though it definitely included poetry.'*

She turns back to me. *'And of course we change ours when we get sick of it.'*

I gape at her. *'You change it? You change the list?'*

'Don't you change yours?'

'Er – yes, all the time,' I say. (I don't want her to think that the ducks of Little Dismal are stuffy. Even if they are.)

'So,' says the great-aunt. *'How about another poem? In fact, why don't we have a whole evening of poetry?'* She nods towards the far bank. *'You could stand over there.'*

I am overwhelmed. They want to hear my poems. They appreciate my poems. They *respect* my poems.

I almost agree to the poetry evening on the spot.

But where would that leave Tracy and Clara?

'What's it worth?' I ask.

The whole flock bursts out laughing. But this time it is friendly laughter.

'She's learning,' they say.

'She's not so stupid after all.'

'What would you like? Tadpoles? Salamanders?'

But I already know what I want. *'Help me find my friends, and I will give you an evening of poetry.'*

Not-so-stupid o'clock

The city ducks have agreed to help me.

But now we strike a problem.

I don't realise it's a problem, not straight

away. I stand on the bank, describing Tracy, so they'll know her when they see her. *'She's human. She has a nose and two eyes. She doesn't have any feathers, but she wears what humans call clothes.'*

I look at them expectantly. *'Got it? Let's go.'*

None of them move. The great-aunt says, *'That describes every human in the city.'*

Oh.

I try to think of something that sets Tracy apart. *'She has hair? And ears?'*

But even that is not enough.

'Besides,' says the great-aunt, *'all humans look alike. We can't tell one from the other.'*

The hope that has been bubbling inside me collapses. *I* will know Tracy when I see her. But I can't be everywhere. I can't search the whole city by myself.

'What about the chook?' asks one of the other ducks. *'What does she look like?'*

'White feathers, wings, a beak,' I tell her.

'But every chook in the city must look the same.'

'There aren't so many chooks in the city,' says the great-aunt. *'And you say she's in a cage? By herself? That's not usual.'* She raises her voice. *'Forget the human. Search for the chook. Come back here as soon as you have word.'*

The pond explodes with wings, as every single duck except the great-aunt and me rises into the air.

I would go too, but the great-aunt insists I stay with her. *'You'd only get lost,'* she says. *'And then we'd have to find you, as well as the chook.'*

She dips her beak and takes a long drink. *'Now,'* she says, *'tell me a poem.'*

Friday
Melbourne

Dear Mum, I used to envy Jubilee, did you know that? She was so confident. Plus she had that American accent, which made everything she said sound like something out of a movie.

Now I don't envy her at all. Cos she really hates her mother.

And she hates having to babysit me.

That's what she calls it.

Babysitting.

'You're such a loser,' she says. 'A boring loser.'

I've gone to the bathroom a couple of times. I don't dare stay in there for long, but each time I lift the corner of the blanket and whisper,

'I'm trying to get us out of here, Clara.'

She blinks at me and waves her wings. I think she's doing semaphore, but I don't understand it.

'Sorry,' I say. 'Sorry, sorry, sorry.'

When I come back into the bedroom the second time, Jubilee's got the TV on, though she's still looking at her phone.

I can't tell you what I watch. It's all just a blur.

Right up until there's a break, and the announcer says, 'News just in. The city has been invaded by ducks.'

I can't help it – I squeak.

Jubilee looks up and says, 'What?'

'Nothing. I – I think something bit me. A flea?'

She curls her lip. Then she goes back to her phone, which is just as well, because I want to hear what the announcer is saying.

'Police stations have been inundated this afternoon by reports of ducks peering in windows,' he says. 'All over the city, in houses, offices and hotels, people have come face to face with these web-footed intruders. But, according to veterinary surgeon Anastasia Black, there's nothing to worry about.'

The screen splits, with the announcer on one side and the vet on the other. 'Anastasia Black, what's going on with these ducks?' asks the announcer. 'Is it a takeover bid? Are we about to be driven from our homes?'

The vet laughs. 'Not at all, Brian,' she says. 'It's been very dry for months now, and I suspect these ducks are just looking for food. We don't usually recommend feeding wild animals. But if people really want to put something out for them, make sure it's healthy – a few frozen peas, some chopped lettuce, or mealworms. Definitely not bread – bread is very bad for ducks.'

They talk for a bit longer, but I'm not listening. Maybe the ducks *are* hungry.

But I think it's something else.

I think Rita is searching for me. And Clara.

I slide off the bed and head for the bathroom.

Jubilee doesn't look up, but she says, 'Where are you going?'

'Um – for a pee.'

'Again?'

I shut the bathroom door behind me, and pull off the blanket. 'Clara, I think Rita's looking for you,' I tell her. 'But she's not going to find you in here. Can you – can you pretend to be sick?'

She peers at me out of one eye. Then she crumples to the floor of the cage with her beak open and one wing outstretched.

It's so convincing that for a moment I think she really *is* sick. 'Clara?' I squeak.

She raises her head, stares at me, then drops back again. She's way better at acting than I am.

I take a deep breath, pick up the cage and run out of the bathroom. 'Jubilee, there's something wrong with the chook!'

She looks up from her phone at last, and stares at Clara. 'What did you do to her?'

'Nothing. Maybe we should phone a vet.'

'Don't be an idiot,' she says. But she looks worried.

So I inspect Clara, as if I know all about chooks, and say, 'She might just need some sun. Vitamin – um – vitamin J. That sort of stuff. I've heard chooks get really sick without it. They can drop dead on the spot.'

Jubilee looks even more worried.

'You could take her outside for a little while,' I say.

I don't really expect her to agree. So I'm not surprised when she says, 'Yeah, right. That's not going to happen.'

'Um – well, maybe if we could put her by the window...'

So that's what we do. We pull back the curtains and put the cage on a little table right next to the window.

Clara wiggles her legs, as if the sun's already doing her good.

Jubilee goes back to her phone.

I pretend to watch TV.

But out of the corner of my eye, I'm watching the window. And waiting for a duck.

Love from Tracy

Frightday

Waiting o'clock

I recite every poem I have ever made up.

Then I make up some more.

A waiting poem.

A wish-they-would-hurry-up poem.

A what-will-I-do-if-they-can't-find-her poem.

At last I see a duck flying towards us full pelt. She circles overhead, shouting, *'I found the chook! I found the chook!'*

I spring into the air. *'Where is she?'*

'Follow me!' shouts the duck, and she dips her wings and turns back the way she came.

A moment ago, I was exhausted. Now I feel

as if I could fly across the city and back a dozen times.

I power through the air. My wings are strong. My heart is brave. I will break Clara out of her cage. I will find Tracy. And together we will return to Little Dismal in triumph.

Half past brave-heart

I am expecting the duck to lead me to a house like the ones at home.

Instead, she flies closer and closer to the houses that stick up into the air like fence posts (only a lot bigger).

'There,' she says.

'Where?'

She points with her wing. *'That window.'*

I fly past the window, staring in. She's right. Clara is there in her cage! And Tracy is sitting on the nest!

They both see me. Clara raises a wing, then quickly lowers it again. Tracy gives a tiny wave.

They are not alone.

I fly back to the other duck. *'Right, where can I find an open window?'*

'The windows in these tall houses don't open,' she says.

What is the point of a window that does not open? I decide to check for myself.

I fly around the tall house until I am dizzy. I fly close to the ground. I fly to the very top.

But the duck is right. There is not a single open window in the whole building.

I will have to go in the front door.

Where's-the-front-door o'clock?

By the time I find the front door of the tall building, I have been nearly run over by dozens of cars. I am deaf from the sound of them, and my feet are sore from the hard ground.

But at last I am here, crouched behind a bush outside the door.

It is guarded by a male human. He opens it for other humans (some with small dogs), and closes it behind them.

How can I get past him? What would General Ya do in these circumstances? I can remember nothing in our lessons about breaking into tall buildings and rescuing chooks.

I will have to improvise.

I decide to try the direct approach. Perhaps the male human is opening the door for anyone who comes along.

Including ducks.

Quarter past direct-approach

He is not opening the door for ducks.

So I try gentle persuasion.

Perhaps-I-shouldn't-have-bitten-him-QUITE-so-hard o'clock

The man on the door has brought in

reinforcements. Now I have to get past *two* guards instead of one. And they are watching for me.

I will have to disguise myself.

Disguise o'clock

First, I need some dog hair.

The city dogs are even worse than the Little Dismal sheep. They do not want to give up their hair. But in the end I get enough.

I find a spot of mud and roll in it. Then I roll in the dog hair, and check my reflection in a window.

Hmm, the two legs are a bit of a giveaway.

I pick up a couple of sticks and tuck them under my wings so they touch the ground. Now I have four legs!

I look exactly like a dog.

It's time to press on with the next step – finding a human to get me through the door.

I approach several dogs with a polite request

to lend me their human for a little while.

Unfortunately, word must've got around about the hair, because they all yelp, *'Keep away from me!'* and try to bolt.

This gives me an idea.

I wait under the bush until I spot a dog whose neck rope is nice and loose. It is a strange-looking creature, with skinny legs and hair that pokes out at all angles.

Perfect.

Its human was about to go through the door into the tall house. But now she has stopped to say hello to another human.

Even more perfect.

'Psst,' I whisper, from under the bush.

The dog looks around.

'I am a murder duck,' I hiss. *'If you make a sound, I'll track you down and kill you. Now go!'*

The dog's eyes bulge. Its legs tremble.

'Go!' I say again.

With a barely heard whimper, the dog slips its neck rope and bolts down the street.

I dive out from under the bush and put my head through the neck rope.

I am now a dog.

Hehehehehehehe.

I am not really a dog. I am still a duck.

This is subterfuge.

I wait patiently for the human to stop talking to her friend.

I wait *fairly* patiently.

Perhaps I should bite her ankles to hurry her up.

But then she might look at me too closely.

I'm not sure my disguise is good enough for a close inspection.

I-am-a-dog o'clock

Her friend leaves, and my human resumes her walk towards the door.

It's not easy to use the sticks as if they are my front legs, but I do my best.

The male human opens the door and stands back.

But then he notices me. His face wrinkles.

'Interesting – er – dog, madam,' he says. 'May I ask what breed it is?'

'Snuffles is a Peruvian Inca Orchid,' says my human, without looking at me. 'A very rare breed, and very expensive. You would not believe what I paid for him.'

'No, I wouldn't,' says the male human.

'I mean, are you here for the high tea, madam?'

'We are,' says my human. 'Snuffles and I are very fond of high tea.'

'Through the foyer to the lifts and up three floors,' says the male human. 'Enjoy your visit, madam. And I hope – er – Snuffles likes his scones.'

I don't know what lifts are. But I soon find out. My human leads me to a pair of shiny silver doors. She peers at the wall beside them, putting her nose right up close.

'I should have brought my glasses, Snuffles,' she says.

But at last she finds a button and presses it.

The wall makes a *ding* sound. The doors slide open.

We step inside a very small room.

My human pushes another button, and suddenly I feel as if the floor is pressing hard against my feet.

I quack with alarm, then quickly realise my

mistake and say, *'I mean,* woof. Woof woof.'

My human blinks down at me. 'Are we all right, Snuffles? We don't have a tummy ache, do we? We wouldn't want to miss out on the scones, would we?'

'Woof,' I say.

By then, the floor has stopped pressing. The little room makes another *ding* sound. The doors slide open.

And we are in a completely different place!

What strange human magic is this? We did not walk. We did not fly. And yet we are not where we were.

I experience a moment of panic. Are we still in the same building? Are we in the same *city*?

I slip my neck rope and race towards a window. And there, flying past, is the duck who led me here. It is the same building, which is a relief. But I am no longer at ground level. Somehow, I have gone upwards.

I hear a cry from somewhere behind me.

'Snuffles! Where have you gone? Help! I've lost my little dog! Help!'

Quickly, I drop the sticks and rip off as much of the dog hair as I can reach. Then I flap my wings until the rest of it falls away, along with the mud.

I am a duck again.

Hehehehehehehe.

They will be searching for a dog. Even if they see me, they will never guess that I am an intruder.

Outside the window, the duck angles upward, as if to tell me that I am not yet high enough.

I think Tracy and Clara must be higher up. A lot higher up.

How to get there?

I will use the lift!

I creep back to the shiny doors and wait until they open. Some humans come out, and more go in.

The doors are already closing when I dash inside.

I don't think they saw me.

Hmm, perhaps they did.

Why do humans scream so much?

When the doors open again, all the humans pile out, shouting, 'The ducks are taking over!'

'Watch out! It attacked us!'

'Beware, vicious duck!'

I ignore them. I am used to the way the floor presses upward by now, and amuse myself by flying around the room pecking buttons.

The doors open and close. We go up and up and up.

At last I am at the right level. The duck outside the window signals goodbye and flies away.

I am on my own. And to my relief,

the humans on this level are not screaming.

Now to find the room where Tracy and Clara are being held captive.

I tap my beak against the nearest door,

and a human female opens it. 'Yes?' she says, peering up and down the corridor. 'Did someone knock?'

I inspect her carefully. Is she Delphine?

No.

Is she Tracy?

No.

I bite her ankles to express my disappointment, and head for the next room.

Tracy and Clara are not in the next room.

They are not in the next room, either.

Or the next.

Unfortunately, the screaming has reached this level. It must be some kind of human sickness. I hope Tracy doesn't catch it.

Friday
MELBOURNE

Dear Mum, Delphine's back, and she brought a man with her.

They go straight to the cage and start talking under their breath. I only catch a word or two, but it's enough. This is the man who's going to buy Clara.

I have to do something *really* quickly. Like get hold of Jubilee's phone.

Delphine and the man go into the next room and close the door.

'Hey, Jubilee,' I say. 'I mean Ashlee. Was that your dad who got hurt?'

She ignores me.

'I hope he'll be okay,' I say. 'At least they got to him quickly.'

'What are you talking about, loser?' She doesn't take her eyes off her phone. 'My dad's fine.'

'That's good. So they managed to stop the bleeding?'

Her head jerks up. 'What bleeding? What are you talking about?'

I edge away from her. 'Nothing. I'm sure it was nothing. The website probably got it wrong.'

'What website?' she demands. 'What did you see?'

'I think it was the ABC. Mum showed me this story about someone getting stabbed. In prison. She thought it was your dad. Didn't your mum tell you?'

'You're lying,' she says. And she goes back to her phone.

But I can feel her sneaking glances at me. And after a while, she says, 'When?'

'When what?'

'When did you see it, thickhead?'

I shrug. 'A couple of days ago. But it probably wasn't him. Cos your mum would've told you. Wouldn't she?'

'Of course she would. She tells me everything.'

'I've been trying to remember his name. The man who was stabbed. I think it was Eddie someone. Yes, Eddie Smythe! So I guess you're right, it wasn't your dad.'

Jubilee's eyes go big and frightened, and for a moment I feel really bad about lying to her.

But I don't stop.

'Here, I'll show you,' I say. 'I *think* it was the ABC. It might have been the *Age.*' And I put out my hand for her phone.

She looks at the door of her mother's room. She chews her lip.

She hands over her phone.

'Wow,' I say. 'This is way better than my stupid old phone. I just have to work out ...' And I let my voice trail off, as if I'm trying to figure out how to find the ABC.

But at the same time, my fingers are tapping out your mobile number, Mum.

'Was he badly hurt?' asks Jubilee. 'What did it say about him?'

'Hang on, I've nearly got it,' I say.

She rolls her eyes. I start typing a text.

Mum its me im at hotel t—

Then the phone beside the bed rings.

At the same time, Delphine and the man come through the door.

Delphine takes one look at me and snarls, 'What's she doing? Zach, get that phone off her.'

I don't have time to finish the text. I hit the send button and throw the phone across the room.

Zach and Jubilee dive after it.

Delphine answers the phone beside the bed, glaring at me all the time. 'Yes … Yes … What's that? A duck?'

My heart leaps. People say that in books, and I didn't think it was a real thing, but it is. My heart definitely leaps.

'Terrorising the guests?' says Delphine. 'Yes. Yes, we'll let you know if we see it.'

She hangs up and Zach says, 'The kid sent a text to her mother, but she didn't have time to name the hotel. Just the first letter.'

My heart leaps again. The text went! With the first letter of the hotel!

But the trouble with a leaping heart is, there's further to go when it falls.

Delphine's scowling like mad. 'Tie her hands,' she says to Zach. 'Use the cord from my dressing gown.'

Zach grabs the cord and ties my hands behind my back. Ties them tight. I try to wriggle them, and he grins. 'You won't get out of that,' he says.

Delphine's still glaring at me. She taps her finger against her lips. 'You've got a pet duck.'

'No, I haven't,' I say quickly.

Jubilee rolls her eyes. 'A pet duck? What a loser.'

'You think it's the same duck?' asks Zach.

'It's too much of a coincidence,' says Delphine. 'It must've followed her.' She nods at the landline. 'The manager thinks it's on this floor somewhere. Grab a blanket, Zach. You can stick it in the cage and take it with you when you go. Get rid of it.'

I can't help myself. I take a step towards Zach. 'Don't hurt her!'

He ignores me. 'It'll cost you,' he says to Delphine.

'If you don't take the duck, I won't sell you the chook,' she snaps.

Zach grins. 'Yes, you will. You need the money to get yourself and your daughter out of the country. And besides, the kid's mother isn't going to work out which hotel it is straight away, but she'll get here eventually. We need to speed this up.'

Delphine scowls at him. 'The original price plus ten dollars.'

'Original plus fifty,' says Zach.

'Fifteen.'

'Forty-five,' says Zach.

'Twenty—' begins Delphine.

Someone taps on the door.

Low down.

At around duck height.

Love from Tracy

Frightday

I-must-be-getting-closer o'clock

Tracy is not in that room.

Or that one.

Or that one.

Or—

Above my head, someone shouts, 'The blanket, Zach! Quickly!'

And everything goes dark.

Night-time o'clock

It's dark, so it must be night-time.

But there are voices.

I don't understand. There are never voices at night – except for the bats and the owls, but they swoop past and are gone almost before you hear them.

No one hangs around at night.

No one except – foxes.

Have I been captured by foxes?

ARE THERE FOXES?

'Help!' I shriek. *'Heeeeeeeelp! Foxes!'*

Someone says something, but I don't catch the words.

Because it's *too* dark. Last night there was a moon, and now there's none.

Why is it so dark?

Have I been EATEN by a fox?

Is this the darkness of a fox's belly?

Is this the darkness of death?

'HELP ME! HELP ME! I HAVE BEEN

EATEN BY A FOX! HEEEEEEELP!'

Someone shouts, 'Shut up, duck!'

That's strange. I have never heard of foxes talking to those they have eaten.

But I won't answer. I'll crouch here in its belly and make myself very small, and perhaps the fox will forget about me.

And the next time it opens its mouth, I'll escape.

Half past desperate-plans

But before I can escape, I'm lifted up and moved.

The fox is walking. Where is it going?

Is it taking me back to its den? Does it have cubs? Is it going to vomit me up so they can chew me?

I never thought my life would end like this. There is no way out. I will never see Tracy and Clara again.

I begin to compose my last poem.

Rita's Last Poem

Remember me, my friends
when I am gone.
Remember me as a duck
who flew too close
to the sun—

(I did not really fly too close to the sun. But poets are allowed to say things like that. Especially on their deathbeds.)

Remember me as a duck
who flew too close
to the sun
and was—

But death and foxes wait for no duck. I'm only halfway through this tragic verse when I am thrust forward, and the darkness vanishes.
    I look around frantically for the fox cubs.
    Instead, I see Clara.

'Are they going to eat you too?' I whisper.

She tips her head to one side. '*Eat me?*'

'Shhh, not so loud. When the fox cubs come, we will attack them together.'

Clara gives a worried squawk. '*There are foxes? As well as Delphine and Jubilee Crystal Simpson? And Tracy?*'

'Tracy is here?' I stare at Clara in horror. '*Why is she befriending foxes? I didn't think she would be so treacherous.*'

'Tracy is trying to save me,' says Clara.

'From the foxes?'

'*No, from Delphine. She's the one who put me in this cage.*'

Only then do I see the bars. And realise that we are in a cage.

Foxes do not usually bother with cages.

'The fox who caught me—' I begin.

But Clara interrupts me. '*That wasn't a fox. That was a man called Zach. You were wrapped in a blanket.*'

Once again I stare. *'I wasn't eaten?'*

'They aren't going to eat us. We are too valuable.'

Of course we are.

I never really thought it was foxes.

'Delphine is selling us to Zach,' says Clara.

Oh.

'But now you're here, we can escape,' she says.

Excellent idea. *'How?'*

It's her turn to stare at me. *'I thought you must have a plan.'*

'I do have a plan,' I tell her.

'What is it?'

'To rescue you and Tracy.'

'But how?' asks Clara. *'How are you going to rescue us?'*

I stare at the bars. I knew there was something else I had to work out.

Half past nothing

There is nothing left.

No escape.

No freedom.

No pond with squishy bits around the edges.

All I have is poetry.

But I'm too distressed to write my own.

'I wish I had brought the book with me,' I say. *'But it was too heavy to carry so far. I don't*

understand why a duck would write such a heavy book.'

Clara raises her head and looks at me. 'A duck?'

'Emily Duckinson.'

'That's not her name,' says Clara. 'She is Emily Dickinson.'

'Don't be ridiculous. Why would a duck be called Emily Dickinson?'

'Because she's not a duck,' says Clara. *'There's a photo of her in the back of the book. She's human.'*

I don't want to believe it. But Clara doesn't tell lies.

So I *must* believe it.

I thought the worst had already happened.

But I was wrong.

Even poetry cannot save me now.

Friday
Melbourne

Dear Mum, I guess you'll find me in the end. But by then, Zach will have disappeared with Clara and Rita.

He's handing over the money now.

Jubilee is packing her suitcase, ready to leave with her mum.

My hands are tied behind my back, and I can't do a thing to stop them.

Jubilee hasn't spoken to me since I borrowed her phone. She's mad at me for fooling her. I think she's mad at everyone. And she's stuck there in that angry place. That mean place.

Kind of like I used to be.

I'm trying really hard not to hate her, but it's not easy. She thinks I'm just a stupid kid with no friends...

Except I'm *not* stupid. And I *have* got friends. Like Rita. And Laurie. And you and the twins.

I wish you were here. I wish you'd burst through the door right now, and save Rita and Clara.

But I know you're not going to.

Which means it's up to me.

'Delphine,' I say.

'Be quiet,' says Delphine. She's counting the cash, making sure Zach gave her the right amount.

'He's not paying you enough,' I tell her.

'Shut up, kid,' says Zach.

'Rita's way smarter than I said. She writes poetry.'

'Yeah, pull the other one,' says Zach.

Delphine pauses. 'Poetry?'

'And she dances,' I say. 'You should see her dance, she's amazing.'

'We haven't got time for this,' says Zach. 'The kid's mother is on her way, and I'm out of here.'

He picks up the cage.

Delphine steps in front of him. 'I won't be cheated, Zach. You wouldn't even know about the duck if it wasn't for me.'

'Yeah, but I'm the one who caught it,' says Zach. 'Reckon that makes it mine, poetry or not.'

Jubilee's sitting on the end of the bed, scowling at everyone. 'Can we just leave?'

Her mum ignores her. She's glaring at Zach, and he's glaring right back at her.

'Ask yourself why the kid is suddenly being so helpful,' he snarls. 'Because she's up to something, that's why.'

'I'm not up to anything,' I say. 'I just want to make sure you treat Rita kindly. I want you to know how valuable she is, so you don't wring her neck.'

And suddenly I'm crying. It's not even acting; I'm just scared for Rita and scared for Clara, and

I miss you, Mum, and I'm sick of trying to be brave.

Delphine narrows her eyes. 'Okay, a duck that writes poetry has to be worth double what you gave me, Zach.'

'And dances,' I whisper through my tears. 'Don't forget the dancing.'

Zach shakes his head. But he's watching me closely, and in the end he sighs and puts the cage down. 'All right, but I want to see it. I'm not paying double for a duck that just quacks and lays eggs.'

I sniff, and wipe my runny nose on my sleeve.

I've done what I can. Now it's up to Rita.

Love from Tracy

Frightday

All-is-lost o'clock

Someone crouches beside the cage. 'Rita.'

I do not look up. I'm still lost in the betrayal of Emily Duckinson.

'Rita,' says Tracy. 'I want you to write a poem for Delphine and Zach.' She holds up a pen and paper.

I turn away from her.

Ducks do not write poetry.

'Rita?' says Tracy.

Delphine and the man Zach are standing behind her. 'This is a waste of time,' says Zach.

'I think she's depressed,' says Tracy. 'Because

of the cage. Can I let her out for a minute?'

'Ha ha, I don't think so,' says Delphine.

'She won't run away,' says Tracy. 'She can't, not with all the doors closed.'

She puts her face closer to the bars. 'Rita, if you won't write a poem, will you dance?'

She is blinking at me with one eye. Why is she blinking at me?

'I didn't know you danced,' says Clara.

'I don't.'

'Come on,' says Rita. 'Just a little dance to show Delphine and Zach what you can do.'

This is insulting. I do *not* dance!

'Why does she think you dance?' asks Clara.

'Because she is foolish. I have told her again and again that it's not dancing. It's unarmed combat. But she persists in—' I stop, and look up at Tracy. Could this be subterfuge?

Tracy blinks one-eyed again.

It is!

I stand up straight.

'Let me out,' I quack. 'I am going to do dancing. Hehehehehe.'

'I don't like this,' growls the man. But he opens the door of the cage and stands back.

Clara murmurs in my ear, *'The girl on the bed is Jubilee Crystal Simpson, the daughter of master criminal Ernie Simpson. I don't think she'll cause you too much trouble. But you must bring down Delphine and Zach as quickly as possible. In case they have coshes or sawn-off shotguns.'*

'You reckon this duck understands everything we say?' the man asks Tracy.

She nods.

Zach turns to me. 'Okay, duck. Let's see you dance.'

Friday
Melbourne

Dear Mum, I'm trembling. I don't know if this is going to work.

I don't even know if Rita understands what I'm asking. What I'm begging her to do.

But she steps out of the cage. That's a start.

Then she just stands there, looking around the room. As if she doesn't know what comes next.

Delphine and Zach are watching her closely. Jubilee is pretending she doesn't care. But she's watching, too, out of the corner of her eye.

Rita raises her wings and begins to dance.

Love from Tracy

Frightday

Dancing o'clock

General Ya has a lot to say about attacking a superior force.

(By 'superior', she means that there are more of them. She does not mean that they are better. No one is better than ducks.)

Her most important bit of advice is, 'Take them by surprise.'

So I dance.

I raise my wings and lower them. I spin on one foot. Back and forth. Back and forth.

Zach and Delphine are leaning forward, their eyes wide, their mouths hanging open.

'It really dances!' whispers Delphine.

Then she sits up with a satisfied expression and says, 'I want another two thousand, Zach. Or you can't have either of them.'

'You've got to be joking,' says Zach. 'A dancing duck isn't worth two thousand dollars!'

'It writes poetry, too,' snaps Delphine. 'Don't try and beat me down; you know you'll make more than that in the first month on the show circuit. People are going to be throwing money at you.'

I dance closer. They are too busy arguing to notice.

I dance closer still.

'Mum,' says Jubilee. 'I think the duck—'

I launch myself at Zach.

He throws his arms up. Too late. My beak closes on his nose.

'Arghhhhhhhhh!' he screams.

He tries to grab me, but once again he is too slow. A quick double bite (with twist), then I let go and fly at Delphine instead.

She's expecting me, but that doesn't help her.

Block, pivot, kick. She falls back, clutching her arm. 'Ashlee,' she yells. 'Do something!'

Ashlee, a.k.a. Jubilee, stands up.

'I'll drive it towards you,' growls Zach, who has recovered from the nose bite and picked up a chair.

Jubilee advances on me. Zach pushes me backwards with the chair. This is known as a pincer movement, and General Ya warns against getting in the middle of it.

Unfortunately, I am in the middle of it. If I attack Zach, it will leave me open to Jubilee. And vice versa.

From inside the cage, Clara squawks a warning. *'Watch out for Delphine!'*

I spin around. Delphine is coming at me from one side, with the blanket in her hand. Her teeth are bared. Her eyes glitter with fury.

A three-cornered pincer movement. I'm trapped. If only Great-Aunt Myrtle was here. I would even welcome Vera...

Then I see Tracy. While the other humans are advancing on me, she is creeping towards Clara's cage. She can't use her hands, because they are tied. But her bare toes wiggle the latch until the cage door falls open.

Clara dives out.

Chooks can't fight. Everyone knows that.

But they *can* flutter in front of someone's eyes until they drop a chair. They can race between someone's feet and trip them up. They can peck ankles like a champion.

And human armies (if they have been properly trained) can pivot and kick even when their hands are tied behind their back.

As for ducks, nothing can stop us! Especially when our friends are fighting and fluttering beside us.

I bite Zach's nose again, until he howls.

I deliver a mighty blow to his right arm. I dive past Tracy and attack Delphine before she can drop the blanket over Clara. I fly at Jubilee with such ferocity that she flees to the bathroom.

The noise is tremendous. Delphine and Zach are shouting instructions to each other. Clara is squawking something about Inspector Garcia's gun battle with Half-Tongue Harry.

Tracy is yelling, 'Leave my duck alone!'

As for me, I'm quacking the ancient battle cry of ducks everywhere, *'Death and glory!'* (The 'death' bit is for our enemies. The 'glory' is for us.)

And then suddenly, we all stop.

Someone is knocking on the door.

'Excuse me, Mrs Cavendish?' says a male voice. 'This is the manager. Is everything all right? There have been complaints about the noise.'

Delphine is panting for breath. But she manages to say, 'So sorry. We were – we were playing a game. With the television on.'

'No, we weren't!' shouts Tracy. 'Help! Heeelp—'

'Tracy?' cries a different voice.

'Mum!' screams Tracy. 'They're trying to steal Clara!'

'Clara?' calls another voice.

Clara squawks, *'Olive!'*

'We're coming,' shouts Olive. And the lock on the door clicks open.

But there's a little chain across it, and the door doesn't open properly.

Tracy races towards it. Zach blocks her. She tries to pivot and kick, but he's expecting it, and he seizes her around the waist and drags her away from the door.

I fly at him and he lets her go, but now Delphine has hold of her.

Someone throws themselves against the

door. Thump. And again, harder. *THUMP*.

Jubilee picks up her suitcase. 'Mum,' she yells, 'we have to get out of here!'

Clara and I fly at Delphine from opposite directions. (Pincer movement! Ha!) Delphine flails at us, and feathers go everywhere.

Tracy runs for the door again, and this time she makes it. She undoes the chain with her teeth—

And Olive, Digby, Mum and Sweetheart tumble into the room.

Sweetheart heads straight for Zach, and they grapple. Mum throws her arms around Tracy. Olive and Digby fall to the floor next to a panting Clara.

Once again, the air is full of noise. Sweetheart and Zach grunt and swear as they fight. Mum undoes the cord tying Tracy's hands, hugs her tight and says, 'Are you all right, darling? Are you sure you're all right?'

Olive picks up Clara and tries to keep her away from the tussling men.

The manager pokes his head around the door. 'Mrs Cavendish?'

Delphine and Jubilee slip past Zach and Sweetheart, edge around Mum and Tracy, and tiptoe past Olive, Digby and Clara with their suitcases.

When they reach the door, I hear Delphine murmur to the manager, 'We're just taking our luggage down to the car. We'll be back to sign out in ten minutes. Wonderful service, we did enjoy our stay.'

She pats the man on the arm, and she and Jubilee step past him.

They are escaping!

I sound the General Alert. *'Enemy activity spotted! Action stations! Prepare for battle!'*

Friday
Melbourne

Dear Mum, I'm sorry I pulled away so suddenly. I wanted to stand there and hug you forever.

But Rita was making such a racket that I knew something was wrong.

She flew out the door just as I realised that Delphine and Jubilee had disappeared.

I raced after Rita.

'What on earth—' said the manager, as I pushed past him.

I didn't bother answering him. I tore out into the corridor in time to see Delphine and Jubilee running full pelt for the lifts.

Rita was flying after them, but I wasn't sure

she'd get there in time to stop them.

They were going to get away!

Then someone stepped around the corner.

Two someones.

Two *very small* someones.

'Max! Cody!' I shouted. 'Dancing!'

You should have seen them, Mum. They jumped in front of Delphine and Jubilee, who tried to swerve. But just when they thought they'd made it, the twins did the pivot-and-kick thing and tripped them.

Delphine and Jubilee fell flat on their faces. Max and Cody jumped on top of them and bit them.

By then, Rita had caught up. She bit them, too. Then she marched around them, and every time they tried to stand, she bit them again.

The twins thought it was hilarious.

You know the rest – how you, the manager, Olive, Digby and Clara came tearing out the door to see what was happening, while Laurie wrestled Zach to the ground.

And how Constable Hennessey turned up in time to arrest Delphine and Zach, and to hug Olive just as hard as you were hugging me.

And how Rita was trying to tell us how she had found me and Clara, but she kept breaking pens – and besides, her spelling is still dreadful. So in the end she told Clara, and Clara tapped out the story on Olive's phone. And I read it aloud.

I thought we'd go home after that. All of us. But Constable Hennessey said I had to stay, because he needed to take my statement.

And you and Laurie wouldn't leave without me.

Neither would Rita. Or Clara. Or Olive and Digby.

So in the end we all stayed in the city for a few days.

Love from Tracy

Satday

Tell-me-again-what-a-hero-I-am o'clock

I cannot disappoint my fans. So while the humans do human things, and Clara finds a spot outside for a bit of quiet scratching in the dirt, I fly back to the park.

The city ducks are waiting for me.

Before the poetry evening begins, I describe how I fought off an army of crazed humans to rescue Tracy and Clara.

When I finish, the great-aunt says, *'You must make it into a poem. An epic poem. Perhaps you could mention in one of the verses how we helped you find your friends? "The glorious ducks of the city, led by their noble great-aunt." That sort of thing.'*

I tilt my head a little, as if I'm agreeing with her. Perhaps I *will* write an epic poem. Perhaps I'll even mention the city ducks. But the words will be mine, not hers.

We move on to the main part of the evening. I stand on the bank of the pond and recite poem after poem, with great feeling. The city ducks flap their wings with approval. They particularly like the poem about despair, and how I slowly sink to the ground as I recite it, and finish with my head tucked under my wing.

As the sun sets over the city, I fly back to the hotel, filled with triumph.

The doorman does not want to let me in.

I explain that he *must* let me in, because I am a famous poet.

He swears at me and clutches his ankle.

I am about to explain again when the

manager comes running. 'Just let the duck in, Danny,' he says. 'Believe me, you don't want to make it angry.'

Then the manager looks down at me and says, 'Um, is it Rita? I want you to go straight to your room. In fact, I'll take you up in the lift myself. And no biting the guests, all right? *No biting the guests.*'

As if I would.

Chooseday

Return-to-Little-Dismal o'clock

It is all very well being a hero to the city ducks.

And to Tracy and Clara.

And Olive.

And Mum-the-spy and Sweetheart and Constable Hennessey and Digby.

But my own family is a different matter.

When at last I land on the home pond, they have already heard the news. And they are not happy.

'You rescued our sworn enemy?' says Great-Aunt Myrtle, glaring down her beak at me. *'You saved her? You were supposed to punish her!'*

'*Punish her severely,*' says Aunt Marcia.

'*Teach her not to mess with ducks,*' says Aunt Deirdre.

My cousin Vera paddles into the circle. '*The cows are saying that you went to the city. I don't know where they got that ridiculous idea—*'

I interrupt her. '*It's true.*'

'*Ha ha, pull the other one,*' says Vera. '*Aunt Charlene is the only one who has ever been to the city, and that was by accident.*'

'*I went to the city and met the city ducks,*' I tell her. Then I take a deep breath, turn to Great-Aunt Myrtle and add, '*Their list is different from ours. It includes poetry. And they change the list when they get sick of it.*'

A gasp of horror sweeps across the pond. Aunt Deirdre claps her wings over her new ducklings' ears. '*Such nonsense!*' she says. '*No one should be allowed to say such things.*'

'*Of course it's nonsense,*' snaps Great-Aunt

Myrtle. *'Also ridiculous and utterly impossible. There is only one list. There has always been only one list.'*

'I knew from the start,' says Aunt Deirdre, *'that we were wrong to trust her. We should have sent Vera.'*

The other aunts quack their agreement.

'Rita is a bad influence,' says Aunt Charlene.

'Not a proper duck at all,' says Aunt Marcia.

They are expecting me to protest. They think I'll beg for another chance; beg to be let back into the flock.

But I have been to the city. I have seen things and done things that they cannot imagine.

So instead of begging, I paddle away from them.

As I pass one of the older ducklings, she whispers, *'Do they really change their list, Rita? Do they really include poetry?'*

'Yes,' I murmur. I look sideways at her. *'Come and find me if you want to hear more.'*

Then I launch myself into the air and leave the pond for the last time.

Home-is-not-always-where-you-think-it-is o'clock

Tracy is back at school.

So are Olive and Digby.

And Clara.

When I tap my beak on the classroom window, Tracy leaps up from her seat and opens it for me to fly in.

The rest of the class crowds around me. 'Rita, did you really fly all the way to Melbourne?'

'Will you teach us unarmed combat, like you taught Tracy?'

'Will you show us how Tracy's little brothers brought down Jubilee and her mum?'

Mrs Savage claps her hands. 'Everyone sit down, please. I'm sure Rita has a lot to tell us.' She looks at Olive. 'I understand Clara will be translating?'

Olive nods. Clara dips her beak into the bag around her neck and takes out her new phone.

'But first,' says Mrs Savage, 'we need to have a quick look at the homework I set a couple of weeks ago. The acrostic poem. Tracy?'

Tracy stands up again and walks to the front of the room. She has a piece of paper in her hand.

She clears her throat nervously. 'Rita wrote this.' Then she begins to read.

*'**F**ly beside me*
***R**est your wings on mine*
***I** will support you*
***E**ven through the storm*
***N**othing will harm you, because I am a*
***D**uck.'*

The whole class claps and cheers and whistles. Clara squawks, *'That is the best poem I have ever heard.'*

I bow, and bow again. *'Thank you, thank you,'* I say. *'I could not have done it without my friends.'*

Clara pecks out the words on her phone. Olive reads them aloud. Tracy hugs me.

Everyone claps and cheers again.

I think I shall write a poetry book.

THE END

Acknowledgements

Huge thanks to my uber-wonderful crit group, who reassured me that Rita's story was worth telling, and helped me get the beginning right. Thanks to dramaturg Peter Matheson, who always makes my stories better, to my agent Margaret Connolly, who is a voice of sanity in troubled times, and to everyone at Allen & Unwin who helped make Rita a worthy successor to Clara. Special thanks to Anna McFarlane and Kate Whitfield for their generous support and vast expertise. And to the marvellous Cheryl Orsini for getting just the right sort of glint in Rita's eye.

About the Author

Lian Tanner has worked as a teacher, a tourist bus driver, a freelance journalist, a juggler, an editor and a professional actor. She has been dynamited while scuba diving and arrested while busking. She once spent a week in the jungles of Papua New Guinea, searching for a Japanese soldier left over from the Second World War. It took her a while to realise that all this was preparation for becoming a writer. Nowadays Lian lives by the sea in southern Tasmania.